Linked, We Soar

A Novel by Elisa Ellis

The characters and events portrayed in this book are fictitious. Any similarity to real persons, living or dead, is coincidental and not intended by the author.

ISBN-13: 978-0986118708 (Elisa R Ellis)

ISBN-10: 0986118702

Dedication

To Jeremy, my high school sweetheart / husband

who has loved me for 25 years.

CONTENTS

Prologue

June

Today is my 16th birthday and I am so excited for my big party tonight. Mom allowed me to invite all of my friends, even boys. I've always been pretty shy, so I haven't really talked to many of the guys in our school. I'm not a size 0 like most of the popular girls in our school. Instead, I wear a size 9, and have curves like Marilyn Monroe. I think my big breasts make me look fat no matter what size I am. My brown hair is straight and won't even hold a curl. I wear glasses but I'm getting contacts today. My glasses are so ugly and I can't see anything without them – everything is a blur. Nobody else in my family wears glasses, so they don't understand how I feel. I hope that my contacts will make me look prettier. Mom always tells me I am beautiful and that my glasses make me unique. I don't know if I want to be unique. Sometimes I feel like that makes people afraid to like me.

I am extremely uncoordinated in sports. I dropped out of basketball as soon as it wasn't mandatory for me to take it. The coach always made me feel like I was stupid, and honestly, I had no clue what I was supposed to do on the court. I avoided the ball at all costs. When I was little, I was picked last on teams for games like dodge ball and Red Rover. I was always the first target of the opposing teams. In 3rd grade, I remember holding hands with my friend, Carla, both of us nervous, as the fastest, meanest boy came running towards our link in the long chain of kids playing Red Rover. Of course, he got through. When playing dodge ball in 4th grade, I felt the sting of the first ball hitting me. Embarrassed but relieved, I sat down on the side of the playground to watch the rest of the game, joining the other kids who were considered dorks.

High school is a lot the same. The popular girls are athletic and skinny. I don't even think all of them are that pretty, but it seems like everyone else does. Carla is in most classes with me, so we just talk to each other. Carla is a lot like me. Although she is shorter and wears one size smaller than me, she is curvy and just as uncoordinated. We are determined that this is our year to shine. We have been going to the local tanning bed in our small town. It is actually a shed in someone's back yard with one tanning bed in it. While Carla tans, I wear my goggles and lay on the floor doing exercises. She does the same when I am tanning. Carla already got contacts, so we are both trying to do whatever we can to look good. We are both smart and do well in school, but that is not what is important to us right now.

Carla and I went to the mall last weekend and got new outfits for tonight's party. I will be wearing a cute jean skirt with a red and black striped tank top. I want to show off my tan. We aren't allowed to wear tank tops at school; we can only wear unflattering, stupid-looking clothes. At least we don't have to wear uniforms. Carla bought a strapless, green sundress that falls above her knees. I'm really hoping the guy I secretly like will be at the party.

Chapter 1
April

"Oh. My. Gosh! That new guy is so freakin' cute," I gushed to Carla after school. Carla, who has liked a boy named Jamie for a couple of years, shrugged and said, "I guess so." Jamie has shoulder-length blonde hair and green eyes and plays soccer. Carla and I don't exactly have the same taste in boys.

The new guy is in the grade above me, so he is probably 17. I saw him for the first time in band, where he was sitting among the trumpet players. I play the flute, so I couldn't look back too much without being obvious, but it was hard not to notice how super-hot he is. He's tall with dark brown hair and brown eyes. It looked like he was already making friends, talking and laughing with the guys around him. He must be pretty confident and is probably going to be popular. All of the girls noticed him! I probably don't stand a chance, but I can always hope. Maybe I will Facebook-stalk him later and see what I can find out about him. I will NOT ask to be his friend though; I would die if he declined.

~~~~~~~

I type the name "Aaron Alexander" in the Facebook search bar. There are way too many, so I narrow the search by adding our little town: Coyote, Texas. I'm hoping he has changed his city on his Facebook page. Woohoo! One result. Luckily, Aaron's page isn't completely private. I look at his "About" section and find out he actually likes old rock music just like me. He doesn't have anything listed about his family, but he has 663 friends from a bunch of different cities around this area. I wonder if he really knows all of these people.

Crap. He's already friends with three popular girls from our school. His "Wall" is private, so I give it up for tonight. I go to bed after finishing up my geometry homework, thinking about what I can do to get his attention tomorrow.

~~~~~~~

Ugh. I am SO not a morning person. I hit snooze on my cell phone alarm clock three times before I finally get up, at 7:15. That leaves me thirty minutes to take a shower, dry my hair, put my makeup on, and pick out something cute to wear. I think I will flat-iron my hair because it is already straight and I want it to be shiny and smooth. I pick my tight jeans that make my butt look good and wear my black Motley Crue t-shirt that I bought online. I try to put my eyeliner and mascara on with my face ridiculously close to the mirror so I can see without my glasses. I can't freakin' wait to get contacts! I throw on my black retro plastic-framed glasses and add some lipstick to complete my look. I really hope Aaron will notice me today, even though I'm not brave enough to talk to him.

My mom drops me off on the side of the school, where the high school is. The school is big, but it is actually several buildings put together. Our town is so small that the school is Kindergarten through 12th grade. The elementary school is on one end, junior high in the middle near the cafeteria, and high school on the other end. I can't wait to get a car so I can drive myself. Even though I won't get my license until my birthday, which is coming up in the summer, I have been driving since I was 13.

Everyone drives early around here because a lot of us live out in the country instead of in the little town where the school is. I actually live about 2 miles away from the school down a road full of cotton fields and a few scattered houses. It is a two-lane highway with most of the traffic being farm trucks and tractors. The tractors pull over to let cars pass, and everyone waves, whether you know the other driver or not – not a huge wave -- we just put our hand up while keeping it on the steering wheel.

I am getting to school right at 7:50, which gives me 5 minutes to go to my locker and get to geometry class. Thank goodness I did my homework last night because our teacher gives us frequent pop quizzes. I hate that geometry is 1st period. I never feel awake that early and it's really hard to concentrate. I think I may have ADD, but I've never been diagnosed. I definitely fit the "squirrel" joke about the dog on the movie *Up*.

Carla is already in her seat writing something down when I walk in right before the bell rings. Whew! I made it just in time. I always sit right behind Carla in this class. Everyone somehow knows that once you pick your seat at the beginning of the year, you sit there in the same spot every day. I get really irritated when someone moves seats. I don't understand how everyone else doesn't have OCD which makes me really freak out when something like that changes.

Thankfully, we don't have a quiz today, but the teacher is teaching a new concept, which means I can't talk to Carla and tell her what I found on Facebook last night. Now I will have to wait until lunch because next period is Spanish (the only foreign language offered in our school), and then we have electives. I am in art and she is in home economics.

The morning has really drug on, but in lunch, I sit with Carla and a few other girls who always sit with us since the popular kids don't usually have room at their table for other kids. Today we are having nachos-- not my favorite but still edible. I hate how all of the school meals now have to be healthy. Does healthy have to equal tasting terrible? I mean seriously, wheat bread does NOT make a good crust for pizza! The only good thing about it is that it helps me to not eat very much, since I am pretty much always dieting.

"Interesting shirt choice, Mia." This, coming from Kinlee, who is in love with Justin Bieber. Whatever. She doesn't understand good music. I like current music, too, but not much that plays on the normal stations. Even though they are very different than the awesome hair bands of the 80's, I really enjoy folk rock and Indie rock. I do actually like Maroon Five and Switchfoot, too, but I have to draw the line with country and rap. I just tell Kinlee, "thanks," as if she is giving me a compliment. I look at Carla, and she clearly thinks my shirt is a hot choice.

"So...I looked Aaron up on Facebook last night," I quietly tell Carla. Obviously the other girls at our table do not need to know all about my awesome Facebook creeping skills and my little crush on the hot, new guy.

Carla whispers, "And......?" drawing out the word for the necessary dramatic teenage effect. I tell her what little I found out and she immediately smiles. "So THAT is the reason you are wearing your Motley Crue shirt? I haven't seen you wear it at school before."

"Um, YEAH. What better time to wear such an awesome shirt than today?" I say, as I look at the other side of the cafeteria, noticing that Aaron is sitting with a bunch of boys who are all talking and laughing. All of the cheerleader/athletic/popular girls are sitting at a table near the boys, laughing and trying to look cute. Aaron is wearing jeans and a black t-shirt. *He is SO cute; I love his smile and his eyes and his hair, and... Oh my gosh! He just looked over at me. Why am I still looking at him?*

I am embarrassed as I stare, in a trance, when thankfully, Carla gets my attention, "Dude! Hello? Look away before he sees you drooling!" I snap out of it; Aaron definitely had to notice me staring, which is not the way I wanted to get his attention. I am so embarrassed. Why do I have to be such a dork?

Saved by the bell! I walk out and keep my eyes forward as I head to my next class, World History. I really hate this class. Coach Martin teaches it, and he definitely favors the athletic students. It seems like every lesson he teaches is related to a sports story. I really don't care about his winning championships or whatever he did back in the day, when *maybe* he was cool. Now he's bald, has a big belly, and lives vicariously through the football boys. We watch boring videos and have to do weekly current event summaries. I want to be informed of major things going on the world, but I really don't care to know every detail, and I hate how it seems like there is so much sad news. Other than that, we do work sheets and take tests on them. My grade in that class is good, but I figure the athletes get extra help on their assignments, so I don't know if my grade really reflects my true ability. I guess I don't really care though.

Chemistry is next, and I don't love this class either. It is also taught by a coach, Coach King. He is a better teacher, and even though I am not good at chemistry, he makes it easier and fun. Today is a lab. My lab partner is Daniel, who loves science in general. I do my part but definitely lean on his knowledge as we complete our work. I would probably blow our classroom up if I measured and mix chemicals.

English is my last difficult class of the day, and I love it even though Mrs. Mac (short for MacIverson) is strict. I feel like I really learn a lot, and she tries to make class fun. As much as I don't want to be forced to read, speak, and write perfectly, I think it helps me to focus and do a good job. I have to work hard to maintain an A, but I feel like I am truly earning it so it feels worth it.

"Open your books to page 97. I will read first and then may call on some of you to read, so pay attention and follow along," Mrs. Mac said.

We are reading Charles Dickens' *Great Expectations*, and so far, I'm enjoying it. I like it when she reads because it is easier to understand. I also like when she calls on me to read, even though I don't usually volunteer so as not to appear nerdy. I try to read as if I'm narrating the story, accenting the right words and noticing punctuation so that it sounds interesting and makes sense. I always feel sorry for the kids who don't read as well, and I have to really focus when they read so I can still understand what we are reading. This class goes by quickly as we are lost in the story.

I am excited but nervous as I head in to band. I sit down and try to concentrate on putting my flute together and arranging our music on the stand in front of me. I share a stand with Cambry, who sits next to me in 2nd chair. I am really competitive and practice my flute daily, even though most of the kids in our small school are not expert musicians. It's something I'm good at, and I feel rewarded when I master a song. I really love playing with the band and hearing all of the parts together. Last year, I made All-Region band. I couldn't believe we could sound so good. That band consisted of all of the best players of the various schools in our region, who were from 1A schools. We practiced for a week and then played a concert for parents and family.

Snapping back into focus, I listen to all of the players warming up: clarinets squeaking, trombones blasting, flutes playing scales, etc., and I groan, wishing the kids here cared enough to practice. I did notice a trumpet playing scales well though, and looked back to see that it was Aaron. Hmmm. I guess I learned something more about him. I hurried and looked forward before he noticed. I did NOT want to get caught looking at him again.

We are learning new songs for our end-of-year concert. I hope our band director, Mr. Cunningham, will pick fun music. Our school doesn't spend much money on the band program, so it's hard for him to get new, good music. I will be very happy if I never have to play, or even hear, some of the songs we did in marching band again, like "Eye of the Tiger" and "Beat It." I mean, really, if we have to play old music, I would pick something way better!

Mr. Cunningham dismisses us ten minutes early so we can put away our instruments, and he doesn't mind if everyone talks since it is the end of the day. I normally take my flute home, but today I go to my locker anyway just so I have a chance to look at Aaron without being obvious. While I'm walking over, he bumps into me. He smiles and says, "Oops, sorry."

I don't even think I smiled back. I was too busy freaking out inside. I just told him it was ok and kept walking. I really need to work on my not-being-lame skills. Back at my seat though, waiting for the bell to ring, I smile to myself and feel overjoyed at having been so close to Aaron.

I doubt he even knows my name, but I'm already writing "Mia Alexander" with hearts all over my journal tonight.

He touched me today. TOUCHED me! Who cares if he just bumped into me? AND, he actually smiled at me too. Yep, I think I'm in love. His smile is so sexy and sweet. I'm sure he didn't mean anything by it, but OH MY GOSH – he could smile at me all day and I would be so happy! I heard that he is in athletics too, so he probably hangs out with that crowd, but I'm really glad he's also in band. Apparently he has siblings in elementary because I saw him walking with them after school. I wonder why they moved to Coyote. The closest big town, Crockett, is about twenty-five miles away so most of the people who live here have lived in this town forever. My mom even graduated from Coyote High.

People don't move here on purpose. I am going to have to investigate this...

For now though, I will dream of Mr. Hot New Guy...

~~~~~~~~

This week has gone by fast. I'm so glad it's Friday because after school everyone usually hangs out at the football stadium for a while before going home. Carla and I sit in the far right, top side and talk to a couple of other people who are in band with us. The jocks hang out on the field and pass the football to each other while the popular girls sit in the middle at the bottom of the stands and act like they are ignoring the boys, but of course they are obviously looking at them, giggling and flirting the whole time. Gag! I've never really been interested in the stupid jocks, but today I'm looking to see if Aaron is down there with them. I don't see him. In fact, I don't see him anywhere. Maybe he had to go home right after school. Maybe nobody told him about coming over here after school to hang out? Now I will have to wait until Monday to see him again.

~~~~~~~~

I love Saturdays! My mom always takes my sister, Lily, and me shopping. We take Carla with us a lot, too. She might as well be my sister. Lily is three years younger than Carla and me, but we all get along well. Every Saturday, we go to the same Mexican food restaurant in town, called Pedro's. They have the best Tex-Mex food, and I get cheese enchiladas every single time, another OCD trait of mine. I also love their queso (cheese dip). It's just us girls, and we laugh at stupid things and probably drive the people who work there nuts. We don't care though. We get sopapillas for dessert, and then we are so full we feel like we are going to die. We head to the mall to shop and walk off our food. I love shopping, even if I can't buy anything (although I much prefer to buy at least one thing). Mom said we can each buy a few new outfits today so I am super excited. It has been getting warmer again, so I will be glad to get something cute that is short-sleeved. We all found some great sales at Aeropostle and American Eagle and were excited to have new things to wear to school.

~~~~~~~

I spent the night with Carla since we go to the same church. Sunday mornings we sit with the youth for worship and the sermon. Then, in the evenings, the youth group gets together and has a lesson. After our lesson, we eat together and hang out. I really like all of the kids there. Since we go to church in Crockett, it gives us a chance to know people who don't go to our school. It also helps us to talk openly without worrying about becoming a part of the crazy gossip that is prevalent in Coyote. I feel like having friends who believe the same way I do makes it easier for me to be strong enough to resist the many temptations and pressures I face every day as a teenager.

"Tonight, we are going to talk about sex," Kathy said. Kathy is one of the leaders. She just graduated from college and is married to Ken. They lead our group together and since they are young, they can relate to us. However, we all feel a little awkward when the subject of sex is brought up. One of the boys, Reggie, starts singing, "Let's talk about sex, baby..." and the whole group laughs. That's when Ken decides we will split up, girls with Kathy, and boys with him. Thank goodness!

I haven't really been in a relationship where I felt tempted sexually, but I do want to look cute and make the boys notice me. Well, at least one boy. Kathy tells us that it's ok to dress in cute clothes that are flattering, but that it's not a good idea to wear things that expose our body too much, or things that are suggestive sexually. She told us that it tempts the boys and can cause them to struggle with doing what is right, and that it does not make us look like a good example. I am thankful that the new clothes we bought are not too revealing since I want to live for God. I leave feeling encouraged but a little conflicted.

> *Dear Journal,*
>
> *Tonight Kathy told us we should be careful with what we wear so that we don't tempt the boys. I don't think most of my clothes are overly sexy, but I do want to look good, and stylish, and cute... How can I get Aaron to notice me if I'm wearing boring clothes? I wish I wasn't so shy. I really want to talk to him this week at school.*
>
> *Please God, help me to be a good person and to not sin, and please also help me to be myself and be confident enough to talk to Aaron. In Jesus' Name, Amen*

It's weird that nobody knows that much about Aaron yet. In this little town, everyone knows everything about everyone. It's kind of annoying.

I got up at 6:30 this morning so I could get to school a little earlier. Usually everyone sits in the old gym while we wait for school to start. Carla isn't here yet, so I sit by myself and draw in a notebook. All of a sudden, I get a weird feeling, and look up to see that Aaron is here, and he is walking towards me. He smiles and actually sits right beside me. *Oh. My. Gosh! God, please help me talk.* "Hey," he says, looking at me. I look up for a second from my drawing and say, "Hi." My cheeks get warm, and I know I'm blushing. Ugh. Thank goodness I wasn't writing my name with his last name when he walked up.

"I'm Aaron."

"Mia. So, how are you liking Coyote High?"

"It's way different from any school I've gone to. I can't believe there are only twenty people in the junior class."

"So, where did you go to school before this?"

"I've been all over the place, moved around a lot, but all of the schools were big, like with 500 kids per grade."

"Wow, that's more than the whole town of Coyote. I think the population here is 451."

Yep, I'm a dork. I just told him the population of our town. Fun facts. Aaron chuckled and agreed. I'm still wondering why he came to sit by me, but I can't exactly ask him that. I decide to ask him about his family, "Why did your family move here?"

He shrugs and says, "It's all new. My whole life is different now. Long story."

Then the stupid bell rings. I hope he didn't think I was prying. We both get up to go to our classes; I tell him bye, and he just kind of smiles and gives me a look like he wishes he could say more but he can't. *What the heck?*

Today we have a student council meeting at lunch, so we take our trays to Mrs. Rodriquez's room, the student council sponsor. We talk about various school issues, but I can't really focus. I sit in my own little world and think about this morning's conversation with Aaron. I hope I can talk to him in band, even if it's only for a second.

I dredge through my classes after lunch and finally make it to band. Aaron is already in his seat practicing his trumpet. I look back at him after I sit down, and he makes eye contact for a second. He doesn't smile or change expressions, but I know he's looking at me. I just smile and turn around to start practicing.

After class, Aaron hurries out of the room, and I still don't get a chance to talk to him. Man! Now I will have to wait until tomorrow. *Unless...I friend him on Facebook. Hmmm, am I brave enough yet?*

Carla calls me later just to chat. We didn't get to talk much at school. She tells me she gave her number to Jamie, and he texted her. She is so excited, and we both squeal together over the phone.

"What did he say in the text?" I ask her.

"How r u?" Carla said she answered him, "Good."

"Then what?"

She said he asked her, "wrud," which means "what are you doing?" She told him she was just sitting in her room listening to music. They talked about different bands they like. Then he told her he would see her tomorrow.

I'm happy for her and tell her about my conversation with Aaron. Again, we squeal. I tell her about his telling me that his family life is a long story and that we didn't get a chance to talk again after that. I hope he wasn't avoiding me. I tell Carla I have to let her go. I think it's time to check my Facebook again.

After signing in to Facebook, I see that I have a friend request, from Aaron. Woohoo! *Thank You God!* Of course, I accept, and look at his wall to see if it gives me more information on who he is. It doesn't look like he posts statuses very often, but a few of his friends have posted things on his wall, just telling him, "hi." *Well, that's not helpful.* I look at his photos and he has a few with him and different friends. He also has one where he is with some kids who I assume are his siblings. That's about it. His profile picture is hot, though. It's just of his face and he's smiling and wearing a red and black Texas Tech cap. I love it and hope to play and march with their awesome band someday, so I think that's pretty cool. I don't think I will try to message him or anything yet, so I sign out and get ready for bed, hopeful that tomorrow will be a good day.

Chapter 2
May

The rest of April flew by, and Aaron and I sort of became friends. We didn't talk to each other much, but would tell each other, "hi" in the halls. Aaron never came to the stadium after school, and I never found out any more information about him.

Jamie and Carla are officially dating now, though. I'm happy for her but a little jealous. She doesn't talk to me as much anymore because she is busy talking to him. I wish so much that I could get to know Aaron a little better. He's just so handsome, and so mysterious, and so... I don't know...awesome.

I'm seriously looking forward to summer. School has been tiring, and it seems like I have a million things going on this month, since it's the end of the school year. At least we are finished with STAAR tests. They are so stupid. I always pass them, but I hate how much emphasis is put on them before we take them. It's like the teachers are crazy and stressed out, which makes them not very fun, which makes the students gripey. At least now, we can all relax and finish up the school year in peace.

Today is Thursday, and our end-of-year band concert is tonight. I hope we will be ready. I have a solo in one of the songs, and Aaron has a solo in a different song. I think that it's cool that we both have solos, but I'm super nervous about mine. I will die of embarrassment if I mess up, even though people probably wouldn't even notice in this town unless it was crazy obvious. We are practicing on stage in the auditorium during class today, so everyone is getting into their spots as I see Aaron getting his trumpet from his locker in the band room. I decide to ask him how he's doing, and he asks if we can talk later, after the concert. He has a car and says he can take me home after if it's ok with my mom. *Ummm, what? Where did this come from? My mom better say yes.* I tell him I will check with mom and see him after the concert.

The solos sound great and the concert turns out to be really fun and probably the best one we've had in Coyote. Mr. Cunningham has really worked with each section to try to encourage and teach the students, and it seems like everyone has gotten pretty pumped up about it. I spot Mom in the audience and immediately go to her after the concert, so I can ask her about Aaron taking me home. She is nervous about that idea, and asks to meet him first. Aaron is talking to his family, so Mom and I go over to their seats to introduce ourselves. We hear them congratulating Aaron on his solo, and then they notice us coming.

I walk up to Aaron and introduce my mom first, "Aaron, this is my mom, Sylvia. Mom, this is Aaron."

They shake hands and tell each other, "Nice to meet you," to which Mom adds, "I've heard a LOT about you Aaron." *What the crap Mom? Embarrassing!*

Aaron just smiles and introduces his mom and dad. His parents seem nice and start talking to Mom about how great the concert was. Mom whispers that I can go with Aaron, so we take off, leaving our parents talking.

We both put our instruments in their cases, and head out the building to the parking lot. I already know Aaron drives an old, red, Ford truck. We head over to where it is parked, and he opens the passenger side door for me. I'm wondering what this is all about. Did I die and go to teenage Heaven, where the perfect guy asks the girl out and it ends happily ever after?

Aaron starts the truck, and we head to the only store in the whole town, uniquely called, The Store. They have like two tables where people can sit in front of the store and eat or talk or whatever people might want to do in such a great environment. Of course, tonight I do not care what kind of environment we are in. I'm with Aaron! He buys us each an ice cream pop, and we sit down to talk.

"Thanks for the ice cream," I say, smiling and then taking a bite.

"Welcome. I know this was out of the blue, but I really feel like I need to talk to someone, and you are the only person I feel like I can trust."

What did I do to make him think that? Of course he can trust me, but I don't feel like I've done much to show him that.

Aaron starts again, "Remember when I said my family and history was a long story?"

"Yes."

"Well, I don't like to tell people because I feel embarrassed about it, but I'm adopted. The people you met tonight are my parents, but they just adopted me last year. I lived in five different foster homes before moving in with them, and my biological parents are not in the picture anymore."

"Wow," I say. "That's good though, right? I mean, they seem nice; so are you happy to be adopted?"

"I am happy, but sometimes it is just weird. They try so hard, and I feel like it will just take more time before I can trust them enough to really talk to them the way they want me to. They always ask me how I'm feeling, if I'm doing ok. It gets tiring. They haven't let me stay after school on Friday's, and they rarely let me go anywhere. I had to ask them several times before they agreed to let me go home a little later tonight," he told me.

"Well, if it makes you feel any better, I had to introduce y'all to my mom before I could go with you. I guess she needed to see you to trust you. Good thing you didn't wear your 'I am ghetto' shirt with red, leather pants today." I smiled and he laughed.

"They weren't clean." We laughed and sat for a couple of minutes finishing up our ice cream.

"So, what happened with your biological parents?" I asked.

"Well, my dad was in and out of our lives, but when he was around, he was always drunk or high. He hung out with really scary, bad people. I think he sold drugs for them. He got the crap beaten out of him more than once, and then he would come home and beg my mom to take him back, telling her he was done with all of the bad stuff. Of course, he would get better and leave to go get another fix. My mom did drugs with him some, and even when he was gone, she drank a lot. She was always too worried about herself and half the time she didn't even notice us. I took care of my baby brother. He was only 2 when CPS came and took us from our house. He had a different dad, and his paternal grandma adopted him, so I don't get to even see him very often anymore."

My heart was breaking for Aaron and for his baby brother. I couldn't even imagine how that would have felt.

"I was in 4th grade when they took me. I had to change schools, and my brother, Adam, and I were separated and put into different foster homes. We were supposed to get to see each other every week when we both had visits with my mom, but half the time she didn't show up for a visit, so that eventually stopped altogether," Aaron continued.

"What were the foster homes like?" I asked.

"The first one wasn't too bad, but it was really different from anything I knew. They were Hispanic, so their food was all different from anything I ever ate. I ended up loving their food, though, and now I can't ever find anything like it. My favorite thing my foster mom made was homemade tacos. She fried up the taco shells, and the taco meat was delicious. I got into trouble a lot in school that year, though. I was still really having a hard time with all of the changes, and the fact that my mom didn't want to even try to get us back. My foster mom said she couldn't handle me anymore, and CPS took me to another home." Aaron said the last sentence quietly, as if he could hardly talk about it out loud.

"You don't seem like a kid who gets in trouble much. In fact, I'm kind of surprised you are talking to me. When you first moved here, I thought you would be friends with all of the popular kids. You seem like you make friends easily and get along with everyone," I told him.

"Yeah, it has taken me a long time to get to where I can talk to people. I have been in five different schools in the last six years. When I first moved in with the Alexanders, we lived in Crockett, and I went to Pecos North. I finished out my sophomore and part of this year there, and then they decided maybe this town would be a better place to raise me, especially since it's not that far. My dad still works in town, and my mom stays home. I have two younger siblings, Eric and Emily. They are the Alexanders' biological kids and are eight and six. They're alright, but they get on my nerves sometimes," he said, grinning.

I asked, "Why did you have to be in other foster homes before going to this home?"

Aaron answered, "Most of the homes are just foster homes and aren't interested in adopting. When my parents' rights were terminated, we became available for adoption. My little brother was already with his Grandma. I was finally placed with the Alexanders."

I tell Aaron I have to be home by 10:00, so we get back in the truck for him to drive me. I feel like he wants to tell me a lot more. When we get to the house, he thanks me for listening to him, but he acts like he can't decide if he should have told me or not. I tell him not to be embarrassed about it, but I can tell that he is. I hope he won't be closed off to me tomorrow.

~~~~~~~

It's Friday, and I can't wait to see Aaron. As soon as I walk into the old gym, though, Carla practically attacks me to ask me how it went last night.

"It was good," I tell her. "We had ice cream and just sat at The Store and talked."

She asked, "What did you talk about? Did he tell you why he moved to Coyote?"

I kind of shrug and just say, "He just said his family thought it would be a good place to raise kids."

I don't feel like it is ok for me to tell Carla everything Aaron told me. I hate keeping things from her, but Aaron was very clear about how he hasn't told anyone else and that he feels embarrassed because he is adopted, especially because his biological parents' rights were terminated. I really hate that he feels that way, but who's to say I wouldn't feel the same way?

I'm disappointed because Aaron didn't make it to school early, and I have to head to geometry now. Blah. I would rather go home and go back to sleep.

We finally get to the cafeteria for lunch, and they are serving a bun with meatballs in hot sauce with cheese on top. So disgusting. I guess I will eat the fruit cocktail on the side and hope it fills me up enough to get through the rest of the day. I see Aaron sitting at his usual table, but he doesn't look up at me. Maybe I can talk to him in band.

I hate how hard it is for me to focus on schoolwork when I am so lost in thought about what Aaron told me last night. I just want to have another chance to talk to him so I can encourage him. In band, we watch the video of our concert so we can critique ourselves. I really don't want to see myself playing the solo, even though I think it went well. I feel my face blush when that part comes on. The other kids tease me and say I'm a teacher's pet. They're so stupid. They act like little elementary school brats. Mr. Cunningham tells me I did a good job and we watch the rest of the video. Aaron's solo sounds great, and the kids don't tease him. *What the crap? Why do I have to be the one to always get teased?* Oh well, it's not like I want them to give Aaron a hard time. He doesn't deserve it either. After class, I think I will finally get the chance to talk to him, but again, he leaves early without even telling me, "bye." I decide I don't even feel like staying after school today. Carla will be hanging out with Jamie anyway, so I go home. I put on my Monster Ballad CD and play the Bubbles game on Facebook. I don't even want to think about anything right now.

~~~~~~~

We didn't get to go to Crockett Saturday, so I hung around the farm all day. I walked to Grandma's in the afternoon, and she made her famous chocolate cake. That cake pretty much solves all problems; well, that, along with talking to Grandma. I told her a little about Aaron, but not too much. I love my Grandma, but I still have to be careful about his secret getting around. Grandma played a little record on her Victrola, and we sang and danced in the living room. I love spending time with Grandma.

I am really thankful it's Sunday. I have really been wanting to talk to Kathy about Aaron. I know I can trust her to not tell anyone, and besides, she doesn't live in Coyote anyway. I wait all day until the youth group meets, and then ask Kathy if I can talk to her for a second. We go into the office at church and sit down on the comfortable couch that they have in there.

"What's up?" Kathy asks me.

I begin, "Well, there's a boy at school, Aaron, who I really like. He doesn't know I like him as more than a friend, though. Anyway, the other night after our band concert, he said he wanted to talk to me, so we went to The Store and had ice cream and talked. He told me that he is adopted and that he loves his new family, but that he has had a hard life so far. He was separated from his little brother, and his parents basically didn't even try to get him back."

Kathy shakes her head sadly. She said Ken was adopted and had some similar experiences. She remembers him going through conflicting feelings of love and loyalty for his adoptive parents, and the same love and loyalty to his biological parents, even though they didn't seem to love him back. Ken had a hard time realizing his true identity, but when he found God, he felt complete.

I was really surprised to hear that about Ken. I had no idea. "Well, after he told me that stuff, he didn't talk to me at all on Friday. I think he is embarrassed to talk to me anymore."

Kathy said we had to give it to God and trust Him to help Aaron to discover who he really is, and to let go of any shame or conflicting feelings he might feel. We prayed together, for Aaron, and also for me to have the wisdom and the right words to say to Aaron when he felt like he could talk to me.

> *Thank You God, for helping me understand a little of how Aaron feels. Thank you for Kathy*

*and Ken, and especially for bringing them to You
so that You could use them to teach us. Please
give me wisdom and help me to be who You want
me to be. I love You God. In Jesus' Name, Amen.*

~~~~~~~~

It's the last day of school, and Aaron still hasn't really talked to me, except to say, "Hi" here and there. He seems like he has been normal around the guys, but he hasn't come to any of the after-school events that we always have at the end of the year. I feel like I miss him, even though I don't know him that well yet. I did notice him looking at me a couple of times, but he always looked away when I made eye contact.

We have a free day in band today because we cleaned up the band hall yesterday. I plan to talk to him, whether he likes it or not. Now that finals are over, I don't have to worry about school anymore. Chemistry was hard. I hope I still got an A in that class. I'm pretty sure I got A's in all of my other classes.

Walking into band class, I immediately see Aaron, and he's looking right at me. I walk over to him.

"Hey," I say, smiling.

"Hey," he says back, still looking right into my eyes.

"So, I feel like we haven't talked much in a long time. How have you been?" I ask him.

"Ok. I've been just been...busy," he said, looking down.

"You know, you can talk to me. I haven't told anyone about anything we talked about last time," I try to encourage him.

He raises his eyes, and just looks at me for a minute. Everyone around us is laughing and playing around, but it seems like we were the only ones in the room. Everything else is just a blur. I finally smile a little, and he smiles back. *Oh my...that smile, and his eyes; they just make me melt.* A paper airplane hits Aaron in the head, and his guy friends start cracking up. *Dang it. We were talking, or at least, I think we were fixing to talk.* Aaron goes over and hangs out with his friends for the rest of the period. I sit down next to Carla and tell her about my little moment with Aaron.

"I'm so disappointed, Carla. I just know he was fixing to talk to me before his stupid, idiot friends messed up everything. It's the LAST day of school. I don't know when I will even see him again," I whine to my best friend. She just nods her head in sympathy, totally understanding how I feel. She and Jamie had a fight just this morning, and she isn't sure if they were even still together. Apparently Jamie told her he didn't want to go to graduation with her. Her older brother is graduating tonight, and she was really upset that Jamie didn't want to go with her. Jamie is really self-conscious around Carla's family, especially after he went to the movies with her a couple of weeks ago, and Carla's dad had a talk with him before they left. "You better not hurt my daughter, and make sure you get her home by 11:00," Carla's dad warned Jamie. Carla was really embarrassed, but she knew her dad meant well. He's just really protective.

Carla continues, "If Jamie doesn't come tonight, it just shows that he doesn't care about me."

I respond, "I think it shows that he is just nervous around your dad. He scared him, ya know?" That didn't help Carla feel much better, but I hope she won't hold it against him too much. It seems like Jamie really likes her a lot, and they have a lot of fun together. I went with them to play Putt-Putt in town one night, and we had a blast. We were all cracking up because Carla took like five tries on practically every hole. On the hole where the ball goes into the tunnel by the water, Carla hit the ball so hard that it went over the tunnel and straight into the water. It was hilarious. Thank goodness it didn't hit a person. After mini-golf, we ate ice cream and everyone put the spoons on our noses to see who could hold them there the longest. It was dorky, but we had so much fun that night.

When the bell rings, I hurry to try and talk to Aaron before he leaves. We walk out of the room together amid a bunch of rowdy teenagers who are thrilled to be out of school for the summer. Everyone is being silly and cheering. I look at Aaron, and he is already looking at me, smiling.

"Is that normal around here?" he asks me.

I grin and nod my head. "I guess there's something about us country folks that makes us act crazy," I joke back.

"Aaron?" Just saying his name makes me nervous, but excited.

"Yeah?" he asks.

"I was thinking maybe we could try to stay in touch in the summer. Do you think your parents would let you come out some? A lot of us like to hang out at the pumps during the summer and just talk and listen to music." I tell him, quite bravely, if you ask me!

He asks, "What are the pumps?"

"Oh, duh!" I respond. "It's by the main road where there used to be a gas station. There are still old pumps there that nobody uses anymore. It is kind of a vacant lot, but it has a street light above it, so it makes a good spot for everyone to get together and chat. It's usually pretty fun."

"I don't know if I will be able to, but if I can, I will," Aaron replies.

I give him my phone number and tell him to text me so I can give him more information. He smiles and adds me as a contact on his phone. He doesn't give me his number, but he says he will text me sometime soon.

Wow! That was awesome! I cannot wait to get a text from the cutest guy ever! I want to jump up and down! Woohoo! I love him!

Chapter 3
June

Mom, Lily, and Carla and I have been shopping and buying stuff for my birthday party. My birthday is next Monday, but we are having the party on Saturday. We live on a big farm, and behind the house, we have a big barn that Dad cleaned out so we could have the party in it. We bought lights to hang from the ceiling, and a bunch of Sweet 16 birthday decorations from the party store. We also got a helium tank so we could have balloons everywhere. My uncle has a big sound system that he is going to bring, and he's going to act as a DJ so we can have a little dance. I hope we will have a big turn-out. We are inviting people from my class, the class above me, and the two classes below me. That way, my sister will have people there who are her age, too. I sent Aaron an invitation via Facebook, but he hasn't responded. He hasn't texted me yet either. It will be the best present ever if he comes!

~~~~~~~

It's Saturday, and I'm going to go into town to get my hair cut and to get a mani/pedi. My appointment time is 10:00 at the mall, so I have to get up early. My alarm goes off at 8:00, and I get up, excited about my day. Mom made pancakes, so I sit down for breakfast. My sister and Dad are at the table, too. *Weird. It's rare that we are all up at the same time on the weekend.* After I finish my breakfast, Dad says he needs to show me how he added some more decorations in the barn. I tell him I will look after I get ready to go, but he says he needs me to hurry and look in case he needs to change something. *Geez. What the heck?*

I walk out to the barn with Dad, and Mom and Lily are coming, too. He opens the barn, and inside is a red Jeep Cherokee with a huge bow on it. Mom, Dad, and Lily all yell, "Happy Birthday!" I cannot even believe it! Dad had told me before that I couldn't have my own car until I'm seventeen. Dad says, "It's not brand new, but it's in great condition. I've checked the engine out myself, and it looks like it will be a reliable car. That way, we won't have to worry about you, especially if you are driving to Crockett or back." I am still stunned, and feeling emotional. I know my parents had to really work hard to get this for me. Since I have my permit, I get to drive MY car to town today with Mom and Lily. I will get my license on Monday. Then I won't have to have a parent ride with me anymore. I try out the radio and air conditioner and play with the electric windows. This is already the best day ever!

~~~~~~~

It's 7:00, and people have been arriving to the party for the last ten minutes. Carla got here an hour ago, though. I had to show her my new car before the party! Jamie got here about five minutes ago, and Carla is happy to see him. Even though they didn't break up, they haven't seen each other since school let out. They go get a drink and talk, while I still have to stay at the door of the barn to greet all of my guests. So far, we have quite a few people here. There are even a few people dancing where we set up a little dance floor.

All of a sudden, I see Aaron coming around the house to the barn. He's smiling and carrying a gift bag. I am so happy to see him that I run up to him and give him a hug. He hugs me back, nervously, but smiles and tells me, "hi."

"Why haven't you texted me yet?" I ask him.

"Sorry. My parents are so over-protective. They haven't agreed to let me go to the pumps yet, and they worry about what I'm doing all the time. They took my phone up for the last week because I was talking to one of my friends from my last school, and it was past 10:00. I'm not allowed to use cell phones after 10:00 at night," he answered.

"Oh. Ok. Well, I'm glad you were able to come tonight," I say, smiling a little too big. I can't help it. I'm just so happy he's here.

We go inside the barn and meet up with Carla and Jamie. They are sitting along the side of the makeshift dance floor watching everyone dance. We haven't had dances at school; you would think the movie *Footloose* was based on our town. Carla and I have been practicing some, while watching YouTube, in my room, but I'm still not very confident dancing, especially as uncoordinated as I am. Lily is good at dancing, and she insisted the party would be more fun if we had a dance floor. I agree that it's fun, but now that Aaron is here, I'm even more self-conscious. My uncle has already played lots of fast songs, so he plays a slow song, and Aaron asks me to dance. *Shoot. Please don't let me step all over his toes, or fall, or anything else stupid.*

He leads me to the dance floor, and puts his arms at my waist. I put my arms on his shoulders. We sway back and forth and kind of look around at other people instead of at each other. Aaron kind of backs up and looks down at me.

"What are you thinking?" *Ummm, like I'm really going to tell him.*

"Nothing, really; what are you thinking?" I ask in return.

He answers, "I'm thinking...I'm happy to be here. I'm happy to be dancing with you. I hope you are having a good birthday."

I feel like I might freak out, right then and there, but I try to get my thoughts together.

"Thank you. I'm glad you are here too. You know, you didn't have to bring a present, "I say.

When he first came into the barn, he put the gift bag on the table where some other presents were sitting. I don't plan to open them while everyone is here. I feel like that would be too awkward with this many people here.

"Of course I had to bring a present. It's your birthday," he grins. "It's nothing big; don't worry."

The next song is fast again, so we leave the dance floor. I am thankful he doesn't want dance to that one. Carla and Jamie are out there, though, so we sit and giggle while watching their expert dance moves. THAT is why I don't want to dance. I know people will watch me and laugh; I know this because I do it, too. It's kind of part of the fun.

We have a swing set beside the barn and people have kind of been wandering in and out of the barn, so Aaron and I decide to swing. It's already 11:00, and the party is supposed to be over at midnight. We sit side by side and swing slowly, listening to the sounds of the party from outside. We can hear people laughing and cheering; I think they are doing the limbo. I look at Aaron, "You know the day we talked at The Store?"

"Yeah," he grimaces.

"Was there more you wanted to tell me? We kind of ran out of time and it seemed like maybe you had more to say," I tell him.

He starts to act concerned. "I did something that I'm worried about. I contacted my biological Mom on Facebook, and now she keeps trying to talk to me. I haven't told my parents, and I'm not sure what to do. I don't want to hurt their feelings, and even though I wanted to talk to my bio mom, now I think I made a mistake. She's asking to meet with me, and telling me that my dad wants to see me too. I guess that means they are back together... for the millionth time."

"Wow...do you think she would leave you alone if you just ignore her?" I ask.

"Well, I was hoping she would, but this has been going on now for several months. I really don't want to tell my parents. Please don't tell anyone. I'm still hoping she will just leave me alone. I thought about blocking her from my Facebook, but I don't want to hurt her feelings either, or make her mad," he adds.

"That sounds really hard to deal with. I will be here if you need to talk about it. You can message me on Facebook if you can't text," I say, hoping he will believe me and trust me enough to really do it.

He smiles, "Thank you Mia. You have been a really great friend to me since I have moved here. You would think it would be easier to make friends in such a small town, but it actually seems harder. Everyone already has friends. It's like they don't really need more. The guys talked to me at school and everything, but I haven't felt like any of them would really be there for me if I needed them."

I'm so happy he feels like he can trust me; however, I can't help but notice he referred to me as a friend. I thought maybe he was feeling something more for me like I do for him.

At 11:45, Aaron's parents arrive to pick him up. He tells me he will see me later, and takes off. I smile and wave, and am thankful for such a great night with him, even if it was just as friends.

Before heading to bed, I decide to open one present, the one from Aaron. I know exactly which one it is because he put it in a Justin Bieber gift bag just to tease me. I smile as I pick up the bag, thinking he was probably embarrassed just buying that bag. I open it, and find a Motley Crue CD. *Hmmm, he must have noticed the shirt I wore when he first moved here. He knows me better than I thought.* I smile and open the CD to put it on before I get in bed. I notice that he circled the track, *Without You,* so I skip to it and push play.

I love this song. I'm pretty sure I fall asleep smiling, my heart leaping in my chest.

~~~~~~~~

Sunday night, at our youth group meeting, Kathy asks me about Aaron, "How is that boy you talked to me about a while back? What was his name again?"

"His name is Aaron, and actually, he's just recently talked to me a little more again. He told me he is worried because he has been in contact with his biological mom on Facebook, but his adoptive parents don't know. He initially contacted her, and now she won't leave him alone. She said she and his dad want to see him. He had told me before that they did drugs and drank a lot, and also that they fought and hung around scary people. I think he is scared that they will actually find him and cause trouble," I tell her.

"And he doesn't feel comfortable telling his adoptive parents what is going on?" she asks.

"He said he doesn't want to hurt their feelings because he was the one who started it all by contacting his bio mom on Facebook. Plus, I think he is nervous that he will get in trouble and that they will be even more protective than they already are with him. They hardly let him go anywhere and they seem pretty strict, even though they do seem nice."

Kathy thinks for a minute, and then has an idea. "Do you know if he goes to church anywhere?"

"I'm not sure. I think they believe, but he hasn't mentioned going to church. In fact, I haven't felt confident enough to mention to him that I have been praying for him. I wasn't sure how he would take it," I say. I tell Kathy that I actually feel a little guilty that I haven't told him that.

"God works in His perfect timing, and sometimes just being a good example of how He wants you to live, along with forming positive and healthy relationships, can allow God to come in and work exactly how He wants to. Just keep being there for Aaron, and if you feel like God nudges you to bring Him into the conversation, then it's time to step out of your comfort zone and do it. Maybe you could start by just asking him if he goes to church, and if he doesn't, invite him to ours. Even if he already goes to another church, you could invite him to our youth group. Ken and I would be happy to talk to him, especially since Ken has gone through a lot of what Aaron is going through now. "

"Thank you, Kathy. I think that sounds like a great idea, and I do feel a lot better after talking to you. I'll keep you posted," I say, smiling as I head back to join the girls in our group.

The group surprises me with a birthday cake, and sings "Happy Birthday" to me before it's time to leave. I love having friends who care about me. I don't have to worry about fitting in or what I wear. There isn't a popular group here. It's just a safe place where we are all like brothers and sisters.

Thank You, God, for my awesome youth group.

~~~~~~~

I got my driver's license on Monday, the day of my birthday. I passed the driving test with a 94. They took six points off because I bumped into the curb when parallel parking. That is the hardest part of the test. Nobody parallel parks in Coyote because there are no places where it is necessary. Half the time, if there isn't a parking lot, people just make their own parking spots on the grass. I was glad to have my own car to drive for the driving test though. Otherwise, I would have had to drive my Mom's mini-van or my Dad's big truck, and neither would have been easy to parallel park.

The DPS office gave me a temporary license that they printed out on paper, and I'm supposed to get the real one in a week or two. It's hard to see the picture on the printed version, but it looks like it's Ok. I wasn't sure if I should smile or not for my picture, but I decided to go ahead and smile because I thought it might look better. I don't necessarily plan to go show everyone my license, but I don't want my picture to be ugly on it. I was glad to have my contacts for the picture too. When Aaron was at my party, he noticed that I wasn't wearing my glasses. He said he liked my glasses, but that he thought I looked good without them, too. *I love that he noticed.*

Today is Friday, and I'm planning to hang out at the pumps with Carla and Jamie tonight at 6:00. I heard that a bunch of kids from school are going to be there, so I'm hoping it will be fun. I Facebook messaged Aaron since he still never gave me his phone number. He messaged back that his parents are going to let him go for a while, so I'm super excited to see him.

~~~~~~~

There are like twelve different cars parked at the pumps, and everyone is out of their cars standing around talking. Carla and Jamie rode with me, and it looks like lots of kids rode together because there are probably around thirty kids here. Aaron pulls up and parks close to where I'm parked. I didn't get a chance to show him my car yet, so I walk over to him and wait for him to get out. He has his music up loud so I can't talk to him until he turns his car off, even though his windows are down. He apparently has to finish the song before he can get out. I don't blame him though; he's listening to *I Wanna Rock*, by Twisted

Sister. He acts like he is playing the drums on his dashboard and sings along.

He gets out and comes over to me, as I sit against the back of my car, smiling at him.

"Is this your car?"

"Yes! My parents surprised me with it the day of the party. I'll give you a ride later if you want."

"Sweet! Same color as mine too," Aaron says, grinning.

"Yep, pretty cool. Red is a good color."

We head over to talk to Carla and Jamie, who are with some kids from our class. Carla greets Aaron, "What's up? Glad you could finally hang out with us!"

"Not much. I couldn't resist coming to see this historic landmark. The pumps look even better than described," Aaron jokes.

"Wow, dude, you haven't been around much then," Jamie says, laughing. The guys bump fists.

Carla whispers to me, "He's crazy, but cute," and I nod my head, especially agreeing with the "cute" part.

One of the guys from school, Chance, turns on his car stereo loudly enough that we can all hear it. He's playing, *Radioactive,* by Imagine Dragons. It's a pretty cool song, and makes the mood fun as everyone stands around chatting. I brought an ice chest with drinks in it, so we all grab a Coke.

Aaron looks at me, and says, "Hey, y'all wanna play truth or dare?" Carla, Jamie, Aaron, and I are kind of off to the side of the bigger group of kids, and we all agree.

"Sure," I answer him.

"I vote Carla to be first," I say giggling. "Truth or dare Carla?" Carla looks at me like she's going to get me back later. I just laugh, knowing she won't embarrass me too much.

Carla says, "Truth, I guess."

"Ok, who is your hot movie crush?"

"Ummm, yeah, that's easy...Josh Hutcherson hands down...so hot!" Carla says.

"Who the heck is Josh Hutcherson?" Jamie asks Carla.

"Hellooo? He played Peeta in *Hunger Games*!"

Jamie rolls his eyes and comments, "So, is he hotter than me?"

Carla answers, "Only one truth or dare at a time, Jamie!" smiling at him. He acts like he is disappointed, but he can tell she's totally flirting with him.

Carla chooses me to go next. I knew she would get back at me. I hope she goes easy on me.

"Truth or dare, Mia?" She drags out my name as if creating suspense. Everyone chuckles.

"Dare."

"Wow, aren't you brave tonight," Carla exclaims. She continues, "Ok, I dare you to scream as loudly as you can, 'I love Justin Bieber!" I groan and everyone laughs.

"Fine...I LOVE JUSTIN BIEBER!" I yell, getting it over with as quickly as I can. The other kids around us look at me like, "You are a major nerd." Whatever. I was scared she would dare me to do something way worse.

Jamie decides he will ask Aaron next, "Truth or dare?" to which Aaron immediately says, "Dare." I could have guessed he would choose that.

Jamie dares him, "Take your shirt off and run around the parking lot screaming."

This should be good. Aaron…without his shirt…I hope I don't stare too much.

Aaron has no problem with that dare. He just laughs, slips off his vintage Popeye t-shirt, and runs, screaming crazy-loud. He's so funny. The whole crowd laughs and cheers him on.

He comes back, and looks at Jamie, "Alright dude, you're up…truth or dare?" Jamie looks a little nervous and chooses truth.

"Have you ever had a crush on a teacher?" Aaron smirks, asking Jamie.

"Heck yeah, Coach Martin is HOT!" We all crack up and tell him he HAS to tell the truth. He says, "No, I can't get my mind off of this hot girl in school who is my own age," staring right at Carla.

She blushes and smiles, while I tease loudly, "Awwwwww."

"K. One more round. This time, I will let Carla start," I say. Carla looks at Aaron, and asks him the big question, "truth, or dare?"

Aaron answers, "Truth" surprising me.

"What is your favorite feature of the opposite sex?" Carla asks him.

He looks at me, and says, "Her eyes."

What? Did he just look at me and say that? Did he say "her?" Oh my gosh! Oh my gosh! Oh my gosh!

Before it can get too awkward, Jamie looks at me and asks, "Truth or dare?"

I answer, "Dare," trying desperately to avoid exposing my true feelings about Aaron.

"Alrighty then," Jamie says, as he rubs his hands together while trying to think of something really good.

"I dare you…to…drive us to Crockett to get a drink at Sonic."

"Wait, are you serious?" I ask. Everyone decides this game is getting boring, so I call my mom to be sure it's ok for me to drive to town. I tell her who all is with me, and she reluctantly agrees. She tells me to be really careful, and that I can only go to the Sonic on the outskirts of town and then we have to drive back to Coyote. The others assure me their parents won't care, and I look at Aaron, wondering if he really thinks it's a good idea. He looks at me and tells me it's fine, but I can see that he is a little nervous. We all climb into my car, Aaron riding in the front with me so that Carla and Jamie can ride in the back together. It takes about twenty minutes to get to Sonic, since it is outside the main loop of the town. On the way, we listen to a mix CD I made from ITunes. It has some of my favorite songs by Poison, Def Leopard, Aerosmith, Whitesnake, and Kiss. I have more CD's that I have made with other bands, too. There are so many good songs; it's hard to pick just a few.

I know that we can't discuss anything too personal with Carla and Jamie in the back, so I ask Aaron if he has plans for 4th of July. He tells me doesn't know yet. He hasn't ever been out in the country where he could do fireworks, so I invite his whole family to come to my Grandma's, where we always cook out and all of our extended family contribute fireworks for the teenage boys to set off. The rest of the family sit on blankets on the grass and cheer for each firework. Grandpa claps and yells, "Alright," and laughs like each one is extremely entertaining. It's really fun.

Aaron says, "That sounds great; I will see if we can come!"

We get to Sonic, and I order the usual for Carla and me: two, large diet Dr. Peppers with cherry and vanilla. The guys both get regular Dr. Peppers, even after we tell them adding cherry and vanilla makes them taste so much better. We sit there being silly, head banging in the car, not caring what people think of us. All of a sudden, there is a knock on my passenger side window. A lady dressed in a really short skirt and spaghetti strap top is telling us to roll down the window. She has long, stringy, brown hair, and is really skinny, like in an unhealthy way. Aaron looks shocked, and tells me to just take off and ignore her. He doesn't look at her. I'm a little scared and don't know for sure what I should do, so I start to back up. I'm trying to be careful because the lady is still close to the car, and I don't want to hit her. Carla and Jamie are asking us what the heck is going on, but Aaron seems calm and just says we shouldn't talk to strangers and keeps telling me to leave. I finally get backed up and start to drive forward to go around the Sonic so that I can turn left on the highway to go back home. I see the lady just standing in the middle of the parking lot still staring at us. It was really creepy, and I have a horrible feeling about it, but I can't talk about my assumption right now.

Everyone is relatively quiet on the way back to Coyote. Aaron looks out the window most of the way home, and Carla and Jamie quietly talk to each other in the back. I'm lost in thought and kind of drive home without realizing I'm even doing it. It's weird because before we know it, we are back at the pumps. There are only a few cars left, and nobody is in them. I guess whoever owns those cars has gone with other kids. Jamie and Carla wait in the back seat, since I have to take them home, and I get out to tell Aaron, "bye" before he gets in his truck. It's not really that late, just 10:00, but we all feel like maybe we better get home for tonight.

"Aaron," I say, trying to get him to look at me. He looks up, but looks very upset; I can't tell if he's mad, or sad, or what.

"What?" he replies.

"Did you know that lady back at Sonic?" I ask him. He looks at my car and sees that Jamie and Carla are not paying attention to us. Plus, the windows are rolled up, so I doubt they could hear us anyway.

"Yeah. That was her, my bio-mom," he says.

"Are you Ok?" I ask him.

He looks conflicted, "I don't know what to think, really. I haven't seen her in so long. I can't believe she saw me in the car, and I really can't believe she came up to us and tried to talk to me. I didn't see anyone with her, but I don't even know what car she had been in. I don't feel like I can trust her, so I felt like we should just leave, but in a weird way, I was kind of glad she made an effort to talk to me."

"Gosh, it's just so crazy. I wish I could take all of this away for you, and just give you back whatever you need to feel normal," I tell him.

"This is my normal," he says, and tells me he has to go.

I rush to him and give him a hug before he leaves. I just can't let him leave without it, even if it does take all of my courage. Thankfully, he doesn't act like I'm weird for hugging him. In fact, he hugs me for what seems like a long time, although it's probably only for a minute. I'm still not quite ready to tell him out loud, but I silently say a little prayer:

> God, please let this all be Ok. Please protect
> Aaron, and help him to work through all of his
> conflicting feelings. Help me to show him Your
> love. In Jesus' Name, Amen.

Aaron gets in his truck to leave, and smiles a small smile at me before taking off. I smile back and put my hand up in a small wave, "bye."

I take Carla and Jamie home before I head to my house. Mom and Dad are still up, watching TV in the living room. They ask if I had fun, and I nod before telling them I'm tired and going to go to bed. I'm glad they don't insist that I elaborate, because all I want to do is go to my room where I can think, and chill out.

~~~~~~~

I wake up to the sound of a new text on my phone. It says it's from an unknown number.

"Need to talk. R U up?" the text reads.

I type back, "Aaron?"

"Yes. Can I call you?"

"Sure. Just give me a sec," I say. I head to bathroom and then grab a drink before plopping back down on my bed in my room. I close the door so I can have some privacy. Lily's room is across the hall from mine, and I don't want her in here bugging me. After waiting what seems like forever, the phone rings.

"Hello?" I answer.

"Hey. How are you this morning?" Aaron asks.

"I'm fine. How are you?" I ask, accenting "you" after the night we had last night.

"I'm Ok. I mainly wanted to make sure you aren't freaked out after everything that happened, with my bio mom and all, you know…"

I don't want him to worry about me. "I promise; I'm totally fine. I am more worried about you. I know it was a surprise to see your mom last night, and I'm sure you have mixed feelings about the whole thing. Have you checked your Facebook to see if she has said anything to you?" I ask him.

"Yeah, I looked this morning. She hasn't."

I have no idea if that's a good or bad thing to him, so I ask him what he thinks about it. He sighs into the phone, "I don't know. I feel badly that I ignored her last night, but I just wasn't sure what to do. I never know when she's been drinking or doing drugs, and I definitely didn't want to deal with her if she had. Jamie and Carla don't know about my situation either, so I didn't want to talk to her in front of them. I still don't want you to tell anyone. I think I am going to wait, and hope nothing more comes of it. Seeing her again kind of made me miss her, but more than that, I felt angry all over again at her. She didn't even try to get us back. How could she not even try?"

"I'm not sure," I tell him. "If she's doing drugs or drinking all the time, I would think that would make it hard for her to be a Mom. Maybe she thought y'all would be better off without her?"

"Maybe...It just really sucks. I hate CPS. I hate that I can't be with my brother. I hate her, and I hate my bio dad. The Alexanders are nice, but in a way I hate them, too. I even hate myself. If I could have been a better kid and not get in trouble, maybe none of this would have happened."

"Aaron, you cannot blame yourself. All I know is that you are such a great guy, and if all of this wouldn't have happened, then I would not know you now. I believe God put you here for a reason." This is the first time I mention God to him. I hope he takes it well.

"Yeah, speaking of God, I'm not sure He likes me. Why else would he do this to me?" Aaron questions.

> God, please speak through me now. I don't have
> the words without Your help.

"God loves you, Aaron. I don't know why this is all happening, but I'm absolutely positive He loves you. You know...I would really love it if you could come to church with me sometime. My youth pastors are really awesome. Ken, the guy youth pastor, was actually adopted out of foster care, too. Maybe you could talk to him."

"Did you tell them about me, Mia? I asked you not to tell ANYone," he said, frustrated.

"It's ok. I haven't told anyone else, and I know we can trust them. They will not tell anyone else. I promise. Please don't be upset with me. I just felt worried about you, so I talked to Kathy about it. She prayed with me, and she said she would keep it confidential."

"Fine, but please don't tell anyone else. I can't handle everyone knowing my business, and I don't want it to get back to Mom and Dad, my adoptive mom and dad, that is," he clarifies.

"I won't. I'm glad you feel like you can trust me, and I will not let you down."

"Thanks, Mia. I know you won't. Sorry for freaking out a little. I'm just so confused right now. One thing I do know, though, is that I AM glad you are in my life, and if all of this had to happen for us to get to meet each other, then I guess I'm thankful."

"Me too," I say, feeling happy to hear him say that, even though I hate that he is hurting. I remember that next weekend is July 4th, so I ask him if he's talked to his parents about coming to our house yet.

"Oh yeah, they said they would love to do that, and asked what they can bring. I can't believe I forgot to tell you that. I asked them first thing this morning. I am really looking forward to setting off fireworks since I've never done that before. Dad said he would take me to the firework stand to buy some."

I haven't asked my own parents if they could join us, but I know it won't be a problem. Our family's philosophy is, "the more, the merrier."

"Let me check with Mom to see if y'all need to bring anything, and I will text you later, if that's ok," I say.

"That's cool, no problem. I guess I'll let you go. Thank you for...everything, Mia."

"Anytime, Aaron. I will always be here for you," I say, thankful he can't see me right now, because I can't stop smiling. We hang up, and I lie back on my bed, thinking about how cute Aaron is.

Chapter 4
July

Mom, Lily, and I went to Crockett to get all of the stuff for the 4th. My uncle usually makes brisket, grandma makes potato salad and her famous chocolate cake, one of my aunts makes homemade vanilla ice cream, and everyone else brings various sides. I think we are bringing fruit salad and bread. I texted Aaron and told him to just bring whatever fireworks they bought, because we have enough food to feed a ton of people. I told them to come to my grandma's house on our farm around 6:00.

A whole bunch of my extended family lives on the farm. My grandpa and grandma have lived here for years. They bought land to farm and as each of their children married, they gave the couple an acre on which they could build a house. There are four houses on the land, all within walking distance, so I have played and walked around this land since I was little, learning what I needed to be safe, since I was pretty independent.

Even though I have never seen a rattlesnake, I was always taught that if I saw one, I should back away very slowly. I actually practiced that a couple of times. I have also learned to navigate the electric fences that keep the cows in different fields for grazing. If the fence is low, I can step over, but sometimes it is a little too high, so I have to get down on the ground and go under. I have only been shocked a handful of times, but it was enough times that I learned quickly that I don't want to be shocked again.

I guess the cows have learned that lesson, too, because they rarely get out. I have stood on one side of the fence from one of the big bulls, and haven't been afraid of it getting me. I don't know if that is very smart, but I've never worried about it. Of course, I'm one of those weird people who thinks all animals will recognize that I'm a friend. I would probably try to pet a tiger.

Today is Thursday the 3rd, and I'm walking to grandma's to see if she needs any help getting ready for tomorrow. The cows are in front of our house today, so I have to go the long way to get there, which is around the field and up by the highway. It's okay, though, because I can check grandma's mail for her on the way to her house. I collect her mail, and head up the little gravel road to visit her.

I don't knock; I just open the door and kind of yell, "Hi, Grandma, are you in here?"

"I'm in the kitchen," she answers me.

I walk up to give her a hug before sitting down at the table. She asks if I want some sweet tea, and pours me some after I nod, "yes." Her tea is extremely sweet, just how I like it. Grandma sits back down and is working on making the potato salad for tomorrow night. She doesn't need help, so we just sit and chat.

"Well, what have you been doing today, Mia?" she asks.

"Not too much really. I can't wait until tomorrow, though. I'm excited that Aaron and his family are coming here for dinner and fireworks tomorrow night. You will like them; they are really nice."

"I bet I will," she smiles. Grandma is sweet to everyone. "They have three kids?"

"Yes. Aaron is a year ahead of me in school, and he is 17. His little brother Eric is eight, and I think Emily just turned seven. I haven't really been around his siblings much yet, but I met his parents at the band concert," I tell her.

"Wonderful. We always have plenty, and I am happy to have them join us."

"Mom said to tell you we will bring some paper plates and napkins. We already got them when we were in town."

"Mighty fine; thank you," Grandma says.

I've always been very close to my grandma. When I was in elementary school, I remember coming here after school and watching *Tom and Jerry* with my cousins while having a bologna sandwich on toasted bread with mayonnaise for a snack. Sometimes, we would all go on a walk around the farm and Grandma would sing songs with us. She doesn't go on walks quite as often anymore, but she keeps herself busy with church and the Coyote Senior Citizens.

I decide to head back to my house after spending several hours at grandma's. Carla is coming to spend the night, so she can go watch the big parade with us in Crockett. We go every year on the morning of the 4th. Even though the floats are usually the same every year, the spirit of the parade is fun, and we have made it a tradition. Our favorite floats are the bands, but the old guys who do tricks in go carts are pretty fun to watch, too. Carla goes back home to be with her family for the night's festivities, so I'm happy I get the chance to see her for a while today.

~~~~~~~

The parade was good, but nothing can beat tonight. I walked to grandma's early, before the rest of my family came, because I want to be sure I'm here when Aaron and his family arrive. All of my aunts, uncles, and cousins will be here, too, so I hope it doesn't overwhelm the Alexanders. I see their Suburban pull up right at 6:00, and stand in the front yard to greet them. Aaron gets out of the back door, smiling at me. It's hard to not be distracted by how adorable he is. I welcome his family and introduce his parents to some of the grown-ups in my family. Eric and Emily run off to play with some of my cousins who are in the same grades as them. Everyone seems comfortable, so Aaron and I walk around. I tell mom that I'm going to show him around the farm a little. I know there will be a long line when the food is ready, and I would rather spend time talking to Aaron than standing in line waiting. We walk around to the back of the house. Right behind the fence that surrounds Grandma's and one of my uncle's houses, is a bunch of trees. We wander thought the trees before we reach the spot where my uncle and grandpa park a couple of tractors.

"Weird. I've lived in this area all my life, but it was always in the city. I haven't been around tractors, at least up close," Aaron says.

I laugh and tell him to climb into the cab of the big one so that I can take a picture of him with my phone. Once behind the wheel, he puts his thumbs up and smiles at me, being silly. I snap the shot and send him a copy. We both laugh and start walking again. There are some old army barracks that are used for storage, and behind that, there is a covered barn where my family used to have pigs and a horse. Now, they just raise cattle. We can see the cows off in the distance, back behind my house. I have to warn Aaron not to step in cow pies, and he just laughs.

"You are really country!"

"Whatever; I love it here. It's so peaceful and maybe just a *tiny* bit smelly," I say giggling.

Aaron agrees, "I love it, too." He grabs my hand, and we walk a little closer to where the cows are, so that he can see them better. *Oh. My. Gosh! He is totally holding my hand!*

"Thanks again for inviting us tonight," he says, looking at me.

We stop walking, and I look back at him and quietly reply, "I'm really glad you came."

Aaron stares at me for a minute, as if he is asking permission to kiss me. I look at him, and nervously wait for him to make the first move. He leans his head down, and kisses me lightly on my lips. Then he hugs me tightly, and we just stand there, holding each other, for a while.

We break apart, and walk over to sit on a big tractor tire that is sitting by the barn. He's still holding my hand. After sitting down, he turns to me again, "I hope that was ok, Mia. I've been wanting to kiss you ever since I saw you in band for the first time. I kept trying not to stare at you, especially in front of the guys. I didn't want to deal with their teasing me."

"You've liked me that long?" I ask, in disbelief. "I thought you just wanted to be friends, and there were a couple of times that I wasn't even sure you wanted that."

"Mia, I just wasn't sure you would like me, especially after I told you about my family. I've always kept my distance from girls, especially since I moved around a lot. I saw you, though, and I had this strong feeling that I needed to meet you. After we talked the first time, I wanted to protect you from myself and all the crap that comes with who I am, but I just couldn't stay away," he confessed.

"Wow, Aaron, I've liked you since I saw you for the first time, too. I kind of didn't let you stay away," I say smiling. "You are not who you think you are, Aaron. You are a really great person, and the things you have been through are not who you are," I add.

Aaron smiles at me, and puts his arm around me. "That's why I like you, Mia. You are so understanding, and you care about people. That, and you are really pretty," he says, looking right at me.

I can feel my face blush, but I try to ignore it. "You are pretty darn cute, too, ya know."

I hear Mom calling me, so I tell Aaron we better head back to the house, even though I would be perfectly happy sitting right here on this tire with Aaron for the rest of the night.

~~~~~~~

Back at grandma's, everyone is sitting around outside with full plates in their laps. The little kids are eating at the picnic tables that are set up. We walk into the house so that we can get our food. It smells so good, like bar-b-que, and chocolate cake, and grandma's house. After loading our plates, we head back outside and sit on a blanket on the grass. We can watch the fireworks from here later. The food is delicious, especially the desserts. We sit across from each other because we don't want to alert our parents to our new-found feelings for each other. I notice, though, that Aaron looks at me with a certain smile on his face, showing me he remembers our discussion. *I feel so happy right now; I could just die.*

Aaron helps with the fireworks, along with some of my older cousins. I sit with some of my girl cousins on the blanket, enjoying the show, and listening to my family cheer for each firework, as if it's the most awesome thing in the world. It's a beautiful night, and I smile to myself, loving every minute of it.

When it's time for Aaron and his family to go, he gives me a hug, and whispers in my ear, "I hope I will see you soon, beautiful. I'll talk to you later."

I hug him back, really tightly, and say, "Thank you for coming. You are awesome, and I can't wait to see you again."

Wow. I feel like I'm in shock. I kind of knew he liked me, I guess, but this has been the best night of my life. Maybe now that his parents have spent time with my parents, they will let us hang out together again really soon.

~~~~~~~

Carla will die when I tell her about last night. She left this morning to go to on vacation with her family, so I can't talk to her in person, but I will text her later. They usually go to the mountains, but they are going to San Antonio this year. I'm kind of bummed that she's going to be gone for a whole week. I text Carla, "Hey friend. I can't wait until u get back – want 2 tell you about last night."

She doesn't respond; I guess she is out of cell-phone range.

Sitting here with my phone, disappointed that I didn't get a text back from Carla, I decide to text Aaron. I know I just saw him last night, but I can't wait to talk to him again.

"Hey – I had so much fun with u last night." I hit send and hope for a quick reply.

He immediately responds, "Hey Mia. I had fun, too. WRUD today?"

"Not much. Carla is out of town on vacation. I will probably just stay home today."

"I wish I could come over. I think I have to help my dad fix things around the house though," Aaron says, adding a sad face.

Then he says, "Hold on a sec…"

I wait, wondering what he's doing. Lily is spending the night with a friend, and I'm feeling pretty sorry for myself that I don't have plans. It's not like I didn't just have a fun day yesterday, but it's summer, and I'm 16. I want to have fun! I hear the swoosh of a new text, so I grab my phone.

"Guess what?" Aaron asks.

"What?"

"My dad said that if I help him out around the house today, he will give me some money and let me take u 2 the movies if I want."

"Are u serious? That's awesome!!!"

"Be thinking about what u want 2 see, and I will pick u up around 7. Gotta get busy – c u later."

"Can't wait!" I say, and throw my phone on my bed, my mind immediately planning what to wear. I squeal and run to double check with my mom that she doesn't mind my going. She already told me this morning that she really likes Aaron's family. She said she and Kathleen, Aaron's mom, have a lot in common. Dad seemed to get along well with Bill, Aaron's dad, too, so I doubt they will mind.

Mom smiled when I asked her. I think she knows how much I like Aaron, even though it is kind of awkward to talk about it. She wants me to talk to her about everything, and I try to do that, but sometimes it's still a little weird.

"So, he's a pretty cute boy, Mia. What's going on with y'all?" she asks.

"Nothing much, but he did tell me he likes me, and I like him too," I smile, a little embarrassed.

"You are being safe, right?"

"What? MOM, it's not like that. Gosh," I say, frustrated.

"Mia, I don't really think that. I just want you to know that I'm here if you need anything at all, and I want you to know that while I don't want you to have sex until you are married, I would rather you be safe if you do."

"Ok Mom. Thanks for the talk, but I promise, there's nothing to worry about," I say, with a touch of sarcasm. I try not to feel irritated with her. I know she wants what's best for me, but she should know me better than that. I ask her, "So…I'm assuming I can go tonight, right?" She smiles and tells me it's fine with her. I love her, crazy as she may be.

After I get ready, taking extra care to make myself look as good as I can, I go to the closet to pick out something to wear. It's hard, because I want to look really cute, but I want to be myself and feel comfortable, too. I decide on my faded, skinny jeans and a cute, red t-shirt that I got last time we went shopping. It's nothing special, but Carla always tells me I look hot in it. I turn side-to-side in the full-length mirror to make sure I look cute from all angles, and decide I'm ready.

Aaron's truck is loud, so I hear him coming before I even go outside. I yell, "See y'all later," to mom and dad before taking off to jump in the truck with Aaron. He is standing outside and going around to the passenger side to open the door for me. *He's so sweet. And he smells good.* I smile at him, and he asks if I'm ready, before putting the truck in drive so we can go.

It's about thirty minutes to the movie theater in Crockett. We chat about random things on the way to town, while listening to the radio because the CD player in his truck is jammed. One of his siblings put two CD's in it, and he hasn't been able to get either one out. He said he was really annoyed with them, but he wasn't sure which one did it because they covered for each other. He's going to have his dad look at it later. He tells me about some of the things they worked on today, a sink faucet that wasn't draining well, a door that had to be replaced, and a toilet that was running.

"Sounds fun," I tell him, smiling.

He reaches over and puts his hand on my knee, and says, "Heck yeah! I wish he had more work for me to do. I can't get enough of being up close and personal with a toilet." He makes me laugh.

"You're so silly! I really love that about you!" I tell him.

He chuckles and says, "What? I was being serious."

"Sure..." I add, still giggling.

"So, did you figure out which movie you want to see yet?"

"Ummm, sorry, but I haven't even looked to see what's showing," I say, thinking I was a little busy trying to make myself look good for him.

"Well," he asks, "do you like scary movies?"

"No!" I say, practically yelling it. I hate scary movies. I scream and freak out like a big dork, and then I have bad dreams later. He just laughs and tells me he would protect me, but that he won't subject me to unnecessary torture.

"K. How about something funny?"

"Much better!" I say, thankfully. We pull up to the front of the theater so we can see what's showing. After picking one that starts in thirty minutes, he parks the truck and we go in. Aaron buys us a big tub of popcorn to share, and each of us a big drink. When we get inside the theater, most of the seats are still empty, so he leads us to the middle seats in the middle row.

"These are the best seats," he tells me as we sit down. I'm glad there aren't many people in here with us and hope nobody will come in and sit right in front of me. I want to be able to put my feet up. After getting our drinks settled in the cup holders, and putting the popcorn in between us, Aaron looks at me.

"Did I mention that you look really great tonight?" he asks.

"Ummm, no... but, thank you."

"I mean, you always look beautiful, but tonight...man, you're killing me."

I smile big, "Well, I wasn't exactly trying to kill you, but I did try to look good."

"You don't have to try, Mia. You have to know you are gorgeous," he adds.

I don't know that; I think I'm pretty, but not gorgeous. He must see what I'm thinking, because right then, he puts his hand on the back of my head and pulls me close to him. He kisses me softly and slowly, and I put my hands around his neck to kiss him back, feeling lost in the moment. I pull back, suddenly remembering I'm in a movie theater and people are starting to come in. I can't look away from him, though. He is staring at me with his beautiful, brown eyes, somehow telling me how much he cares for me, without saying anything at all. I smile and then rest my head on his shoulder.

"Thank you."

"For what, kissing you?" he asks.

I giggle and tell him, "No, for taking me here tonight, and just for being so sweet to me."

The movie is starting, so we can't talk out loud anymore. Aaron has his arm around me, and I snuggle up to him, so comfortable, as we enjoy laughing together at the crazy movie we picked.

After the movie, we jump back into the truck, and Aaron pats the spot right next to where he is sitting.

"Scoot over here."

I smile and scoot closer to him, and use the middle seat belt to get buckled. I love being close to him. I can still smell his soap, or shampoo, or whatever it is that makes him smell so good. We decide to go to McDonald's to grab a hamburger before going home. We stop at the one outside of the loop because it is on the way back to Coyote, along the main highway. There are kind of a lot of people here even though it is late, but we go in and order before choosing a booth in the corner. Maybe it won't be quite as hectic and loud in the corner booth, since the place is pretty full. I got a Happy Meal, and Aaron is playing with the miniature robot guy and is talking like a robot, "You. Are. So. Hot. Give. Me. A. Kiss." I laugh and grab the robot and give it a kiss. Aaron chuckles and says, "My turn...give ME a kiss, now." I turn to him and give him a kiss, and even though it's a short kiss, it is sweet, and we both smile at each other, probably looking very dorky to the people in the restaurant. Because we are so focused on each other, we don't notice her at first. All of a sudden, his bio mom sits in the booth seat across the table from us.

"Hi Aaron. You want to introduce me to your friend?" she asks, looking at me.

Aaron squeezes my hand; I don't even know if he realizes he's doing it. I just squeeze it back, to attempt to calm him a little.

"What are you doing here, Mom? How did you know I was here?" Aaron asks her.

"Good to see you too, Aaron. I live in this area. You would know that if you weren't living with some strangers, acting like you are too good to be my son."

I cringe and wonder how he can even feel anything for her, and can't help but to say, "Aaron is such a great guy. You should be so proud of him."

"You don't know Aaron like I do then. Aaron, did you tell your little friend about all of the bad things you used to do?"

Aaron looks uncomfortable and sad and furious all at the same time. "You need to leave now. I don't know why you are acting like this. You never took care of Adam and me. We were alone most of the time. Just pretend we never existed. That's how you acted when we lived with you anyway. I'm sorry I contacted you, and I won't do it again. I thought maybe you would have changed."

"Wait," she says, as she grabs Aaron's arm. "I'm sorry. I screwed up, as usual. I just hate seeing you live your life as if you are a different person now. You need to remember where you came from, Aaron."

At that, we get up and leave. Aaron didn't say anything else to her and thankfully, she didn't follow us to the truck. We get back in the truck, and I automatically sit close to Aaron, in the middle seat.

"Are you ok?" I ask him.

"Not really, but I guess it doesn't matter. She was drunk. I'm really sorry you had to see that. She wasn't always like that. Sometimes, when she was sober, she was loving to Adam and me."

"Aaron, I'm kind of worried that she isn't going to leave you alone. Maybe you should tell your parents. I'm sure they would..."

"No! And you don't tell either. We just have to put it behind us. They don't need to know or be involved because I'm sure nothing more will come of it."

"I'm sorry. I understand...I won't tell," I say, feeling a little upset that he raised his voice.

"No; I'm sorry, Mia. I just get so mad. I don't mean to take it out on you, though. Come here," he says, putting his hand on my head to bring me even closer to him. He grabs my hand, and uses his left hand to steer, as he drives me home. We listen to the radio quietly, and ride the rest of the way without talking.

At home, Aaron kisses me goodnight, and tells me he is sorry again. I'm not mad at him, though. I'm just worried about him. I hug him and then wave, "bye," as I look back from the porch, before I open the door to go inside.

~~~~~~~

I texted Aaron this morning to see if he could come to our youth group tonight, but he said he couldn't make it tonight. I wonder if he just doesn't want to go.

I talked to Kathy tonight and told her about us seeing Aaron's bio mom again. I relayed the conversation to her, and Kathy said that Aaron's bio mom is probably blaming Aaron because she can't handle the pain and pressure of accepting responsibility for her actions. If she defers the blame, she doesn't have to feel the guilt. Kathy encouraged me to keep praying for Aaron, and also for his bio mom.

"How can I pray for his bio mom? She was so mean to Aaron. He's the one who is being mistreated," I say, feeling confused.

"You can still pray for her. Everyone needs God. You can pray that she will find God and that she will be healed from her addictions," Kathy clarifies.

"Ok. It's just hard, because she made me so angry with the way she talked to him. I will pray for both of them, though."

"That's all you can do right now. God is in control, and He will help you be a good support person for Aaron. Hopefully, Aaron will eventually come join us. We would love to talk with him."

"I hope so, too. Thank you, Kathy."

~~~~~~~

Carla finally texted me back. She is on her way back home.

"Dude! Tell me everything!"

I giggle, excited to tell Carla about everything that has happened with Aaron. I just have to keep part of it secret. "It will take 4ever 2 tell u on a text. When r u getting back?"

"Actually, we r about 2 hours away. Maybe I can go 2 ur house 2night. Will ask mom." Carla knows that we are welcome at each other's houses pretty much anytime. I know my mom won't mind if Carla comes over, but we always ask to be sure, and also to be respectful.

Carla gets to my house just after supper, and we go to my room so we can talk. I'm so happy to be able to tell her about Aaron.

"So…first of all, you know Aaron and his family came for 4th of July. Well, I showed him around the farm before supper, and he held my hand while we walked. Then, he told me he likes me, and kissed me!"

"I KNEW he liked you!" Carla squeals!

"I thought he might like me, too, but he told me he has actually liked me a long time. He even told me that I'm pretty. I was so excited."

"That's awesome, Mia! Maybe we can all double date soon. I'm dying to see Jamie. Maybe we could hang out at the pumps again on Friday. That was so fun last time!"

"I really hope so, too! Anyway, that's not even everything," I say, smiling because I haven't even told her about my date with Aaron to the movies yet.

"What? What else happened?" she asks.

"Well, on Saturday, Aaron took me to a movie!" I say excitedly, as if I've won the lottery.

"Are you serious? You went on a date? I can't believe it! I bet it was freakin' awesome!"

"It was. I sat right next to him in his truck. We kissed several times, and he was so sweet. He had his arm around me during the whole movie. Oh, and I was wearing that cute, red shirt that you have always liked, and he said I looked gorgeous!" I tell her, dreamily. "We've texted some since then, but it would be so cool if we could see each other again on Friday. I miss him."

"I totally understand! Everything is so great right now for both of us," Carla says, and we hug each other in celebration.

We go to the kitchen to get some chips and salsa and Diet Dr. Peppers before sitting on bean bags in my bedroom floor. We get comfy and put on the movie, *Twilight,* to be followed by the rest of the series, since I have them all on DVD. I'm Team Edward and Carla is Team Jacob, so we enjoy teasing each other throughout the movie. "Edward is so hot!" I tell her.

"No he isn't. He's overly white and skinny. Plus, he's cold, literally. Jacob is the HOT one," Carla argues.

"If you like dogs..." I tease her.

All of a sudden, we hear a knock on my bedroom window. We both scream, but my door is closed so I don't think my parents hear us. We are freaking out, and I'm about to go get my Dad, when we hear another knock, but it's in a playful pattern. Then we hear someone quietly say, "Hey, it's us. Look out your window."

We peek out the edge of the curtain, hoping they can't see us, but they immediately look to where we are. It's Aaron and Jamie. They are both standing outside the window, smiling at us. We squeal and open the window just a little.

"What are y'all doing? Are you crazy? How did y'all get here without anyone hearing you?" I ask them a million questions, a little nervous that we will get in trouble.

Aaron answers, "I spent the night with Jamie, and he knew Carla was here, so we decided to come see y'all. Do you think y'all could come out? We could walk around with all of the cows and hope we don't step in anything gross."

Carla and I both giggle, knowing we would have to use moonlight to watch where we step. It's 11:00, and I'm scared about sneaking out. I've always been a rule follower, and I really don't want to make my parents mad, or upset with me.

Carla says, "Come on, Mia. We'll just stay out for a little bit. It will be fine."

The guys both chime in, "Yeah, come on, Mia. We aren't vampires or anything." Carla and I both laugh since we were just watching *Twilight*.

"Fine," I say, "but only for like thirty minutes."

Carla and I put our shoes on and crawl out the window. We close it back most of the way but leave it open a crack so that we can easily get back in. We can hear crickets and frogs making sounds. We have a little lake a ways back behind my house. It is only full when it has rained a lot, and we have had several storms recently. We give the guys hugs, and decide to walk over and sit on the tire where Aaron and I sat on the 4th, when I was showing him the cows and the farm. Hopefully, the cows aren't too close. We climb over the electric fence that goes between my house and the barn behind Grandma's house, the guys holding our hands to steady us and help us over so that we don't get shocked. Successfully making it over the fence, we walk to where the big tractor tire sits. We all sit down, and just chat. We try to talk quietly, not wanting anyone to catch us. It feels nerve-wracking, but exhilarating to be out with the boys when we aren't supposed to. I justify it, though, because we aren't really doing anything wrong. However, after we've been out for thirty minutes, I remind everyone that we should get back, so we get up to head back to the house. Carla and Jamie hang back a little, so they can have more privacy.

Aaron holds my hand, and when we stop back by the window, he faces me. "You know, we've been hanging out and everything…and have kissed and stuff. I was just wondering, though, if you want to make it official."

"Are you saying you want me to be your girlfriend?" I say, smiling at him.

"Yes, if you want to."

"Ummmmm, let me think about it….. ummmmmm, of course I want to be your girlfriend!"

"Thanks for keeping me in suspense," Aaron jokes back, smiling at my silly attempt to tease him.

"Anytime, boyfriend!" I say, testing out the word.

"You are so adorable, Mia. You've made me really happy! I wish I didn't have to leave right now." He kisses me so sweetly, and then we stand there hugging until Jamie and Carla have caught up to us. We tell the boys, "bye," and crawl back through my window. My parents seem to still be asleep, so we breathe a sigh of relief, and whisper to each other late into the night about how much fun we had with our cute boyfriends.

~~~~~~~

It's Friday, and Carla and I are meeting Jamie and Aaron at the pumps tonight. After picking Carla up from her house, I drive to the pumps and park. There are only a few people here, nobody that we usually hang out with because they are older. Carla and I check our makeup in our visor mirrors while waiting for the guys to arrive. Our parents have agreed to allow us to go into town tonight, so when the guys get here, they join us in my car, since I have a backseat. Like the last time we hung out together, Jamie and Carla jump in the back, allowing Aaron to ride up front with me.

"Hey babe," Aaron greets me. I love the new pet name he has given me.

"Hi, my handsome boyfriend."

Aaron looks back at Carla, and asks us if we have picked a place to go for dinner.

"Where do y'all want to go?" We revert the question back to him.

Jamie chides in from the back seat, "How about the place where the waitresses are dressed in bikinis?"

"Ha ha; real funny!" Carla smacks Jamie's arm.

"What? What's wrong with that?" Jamie asks innocently. Smack. Carla smacks Jamie's arm again and tells him to stop teasing us.

"Maybe WE should decide, Mia," Carla says to me, "since apparently my boyfriend can't think of a good place!" Aaron and I laugh at Carla and Jamie as they pick on each other playfully.

"Ok. How about that new Italian restaurant by the mall?" I suggest.

Everyone agrees, and we are all thankful that the wait isn't too long. We get seated in a very nice room that has lights strung along the ceiling and candles on the tables. Romantic music creates an inviting atmosphere for our double date. I put my napkin in my lap, and look at the menu. The guys have said they would pay for our meal, so I try not to pick the most expensive item. The chicken parmesan isn't too pricey, and it's my favorite anyway, so I put my menu down, ready to order. By the time the waiter returns, we are all ready to order, so he writes down what we want in his little notebook, and leaves us with a basket of garlic bread sticks. It's a good thing, because we are starving, and it tides us over until our food arrives. We laugh as the guys simulate a little swordfight with their breadsticks. Thankfully, we are in a corner where we aren't too noticeable to everyone else.

Dinner is delicious and everyone is full, but not too full for the chocolate mint we get upon leaving. Back in the car, we decide to hang out at the park before heading back to Coyote. We go to a park that happens to have four swings, and there is no one here since it's almost dark. We swing, all side-by-side, enjoying the competition between Aaron and Jamie, as they see who can swing the highest. When it finally gets all the way dark, we pile back into the car and head home. It's been so much fun, and for once, we have had a great night in Crockett without being interrupted by Aaron's bio mom. Hopefully, she will not show up again.

We park back at the pumps and all get out. We don't want this night to end, and we don't have to be home for another forty-five minutes, so we decide to just hang out there and chat.

"I had a lot of fun tonight, Aaron. Thank you for dinner. I loved that place; it was so romantic," I tell him.

"You are welcome! I would be happy anywhere as long as you are with me." He kisses me and gives me a hug. *I love the sweet things he says to me.* We hold hands and talk about random things until it's time for me to go. Carla and I leave in my car at the same time that the guys leave, and I drive to my house, since Carla is spending the night with me again.

The next two weeks are wonderful; I am constantly talking to or texting Aaron, and we've hung out a little a couple more times at the pumps, the school playground, and one time we just walked around our little town. It has been perfect, and definitely the best summer I have ever had.

Chapter 5
August

I can't believe school starts back in three weeks. We will start practicing for marching band a week before the first day back, so it feels like we only have two weeks left of summer. In a way, I wish we had longer to relax and do nothing. However, I am kind of ready to go back because even though Aaron will be a senior and I will be a junior, we will still see each other every day at school. We will be in band together again, and I plan to get to school early so I can see him before class, and then we will have lunch together, too. For this last couple of weeks though, I plan to spend as much time as possible with him. His parents have definitely lightened up and have allowed him to leave home to hang around me and sometimes Jamie and Carla. He's supposed to eat dinner with my family tonight. My dad is grilling steak and mom is baking potatoes and putting together a salad. This is my favorite meal. I even made my grandma's chocolate cake earlier today so we will have dessert.

We usually eat at the table at our house, especially on weekends. Once school starts, Lily and I will be busy some nights, so my parents insist we sit together for at least one meal a day. Aaron sits beside me, Mom and Lily across from us, and Dad always sits at the head of the table.

"Glad you could join us for dinner tonight, Aaron," Dad tells him.

Aaron smiles, "Thank you for having me. It looks great!"

"How are your parents doing? We need to have your whole family over again sometime."

"They are doing fine. Eric and Emily drive me nuts, but they are good kids," Aaron chuckles.

Mom enters in, "Isn't that what younger siblings are for?" laughing with Aaron.

"That's what my younger sibling is for," I say, smiling at Lily.

"Hey, you are the annoying one, not me!" Lily jokes back.

Dad changes the subject, and we all discuss school starting soon. Aaron is excited to be a senior, and is looking forward to football season. I've never seen him play because he moved to Coyote in the spring, so I'm pretty excited to have my boyfriend playing with our team. I will be at every game with the band, so I will be able to watch him. *I bet he will look hot in his football uniform!* Dad forces Aaron to eat more steak, practically taunting him, "You can eat more; you're a growing, teenage boy!" Aaron eats it, but when he's finished, I can tell he's really full. He still has a little room for cake though. Grandma's chocolate cake is impossible to turn down.

After dinner, we sit on the couch together, holding hands, while watching a movie with my family. I see my parents look at us, so I know they notice us holding hands. I don't think it bothers them, but I sure wouldn't want to kiss in front of my parents. They are still pretty protective, and I don't exactly want to encourage mom to give me another "talk."

Aaron lives about five miles from us. After taking our road to the main highway, he only has to go about four more miles before he's home. His curfew tonight is 11:00, so he waits until the last minute before leaving, at 10:53, giving him a few minutes to get in and out of the car. I walk him out to his truck and give him a kiss before he has to go.

"I'll text you when I get home to let you know I made it."

"K. Can't wait to see you again. Thank you for enduring my crazy family," I joke.

"Anytime. You are a part of that family, ya know. I want to be where you are." He smiles as he gets into his truck to leave, and we wave to each other before I go in.

I get ready for bed, and wait for Aaron's "goodnight" text. It's been twenty minutes, so I decide to text him, assuming he forgot to text me. He responds, "Can't talk."

What the heck? Everything was fine when he left. I hope he's ok.

"Are u Ok?"

"Not really. Apparently my bio mom contacted my adopted mom on Facebook tonight. Not good. Will fill u in 2morrow."

Crap. I wonder what she said to them. God, please be with Aaron and his family. In Jesus' Name, Amen.

~~~~~~~

It's been a week and a half since Aaron came over for supper, and I still haven't heard from him. I keep trying to text and call him, but his phone goes straight to voice mail every time and he hasn't responded. I'm feeling worried about him. I tried to message him on Facebook, but his page is gone. *What the crap?* If I don't hear from him soon, I'm going to freak out. I decided to tell my mom about Aaron being adopted and about his bio mom contacting the Alexanders. I just really need to tell someone, and Mom always has good advice.

"Wow, I had no idea. Aaron even looks like the Alexanders," Mom exclaimed.

"I know. They are really nice, and he loves them, but he's been feeling conflicted about his bio mom contacting him. I think he still loves her even though she has been so horrible to him."

"I'm sure he does still love her. He probably always will. He may just have to let her go, though, because it sounds like she is still struggling with whatever issues caused her to lose him. He's adopted now, and the Alexanders love him."

"Yeah, I agree. The thing is, Aaron's parents moved to Coyote to protect him and raise him in a good environment. They were finally giving him a little freedom to have fun, and now, I'm afraid they will be really strict again."

"There may be more to it than we know, though, Mia. We don't even know what his bio mom said to the Alexanders, so they may have good reason to be protective," Mom says.

"But how can they not at least let him talk to me? I'm his girlfriend!" I start to cry and Mom hugs me.

"Honey, it'll blow over and get better. I'm sure of it. We'll just keep praying for all of them."

I go to my room to chill out and write in my journal. It always makes me feel better. I listen to the CD that Aaron gave me for my birthday while I write.

> *Dear Journal,*
>
> *I hate this. I haven't heard from Aaron in a whole week and a half. His stupid bio mom got in touch with Aaron's mom, and now I can't reach him at all. I don't know if he's ignoring me, or if they aren't letting him talk to me. Why wouldn't they let him talk to me, though? It's not like I am going to hurt him. And what if he is ignoring me? Dinner went well, and everything seemed ok when he left the other night. I keep going back*

through that night to remember if there was anything that was weird about it. I really don't think so, though. We had a great night. I remember when he first told me about being adopted, he kind of ignored me at school for a while. I sure hope that's not the case now. Surely, he knows I don't judge him. Ugh. I don't know what to think.

Please God, please let everything be ok with Aaron and his family. Please let me hear from him soon. I need to know he's ok. Thank You God. In Jesus' Name, Amen.

~~~~~~~~

It's Sunday and we are having a back to school bash with the youth. I have to bring chips and dip. Everyone is bringing something different so that we can snack and play games. Our youth group has about twenty kids in it normally, but tonight there are maybe ten visitors. We were all encouraged to invite a friend. Too bad my "friend" couldn't be here. I still haven't heard from Aaron, and I was hoping he could have come with me to this party. I feel disappointed. Carla has been asking me what is going on, and I still don't think I can tell anyone, so I've just told her he's been busy. I really hate lying to her, and it would be nice if I could talk to her about everything. I just don't feel like it's a good idea yet. I'm kind of tired of talking about it with Kathy. I don't have anything new to tell her since last week, and it just makes me sad to even think about him. Kathy tells me that she and Ken are continuing to pray, so I figure that's the best anyone can do right now.

Carla and I are partners for most of the games. With both of us being crazy uncoordinated, we haven't won a game yet, but I have to admit, it was pretty hilarious to attempt to run with each of us having one leg in a sack for the sack race. We only fell a few times, and I'm pretty sure some people finished before we even made it half-way. Then, when we played a whipped cream game, we both ended up with it all over us. It might as well have been a food fight. We had a lot of fun, though. It's nice to have a stress-free night; I have been so overwhelmed with worrying about Aaron, and now with band practice and school starting soon, I have been freaking out a little.

Tomorrow is our first band practice and I'm wondering if Aaron will be there. I don't know if he has to attend since he's in football. The football kids used to march during half-time with their football uniforms on, but I think the coaches have told them they need to be in the locker room with the other players from now on. *Oh, how I wish he would be there though, just so I could see him.*

~~~~~~~

I've practiced my flute some during the summer, but not as much as I probably should have been. I hope I will not sound awful during practice. When I get to the field, I see that we are just practicing basic marching skills right now, so we don't need our instruments yet. I'm thankful for that, but it's still crazy hot outside, even though it's already 6:00 in the evening. Our weather has been crazy as usual this year. We have had several major thunderstorms that are preceded by enormous dust storms and occasional tornados. Everyone in this area knows what to do in case of a tornado, since we are in tornado alley. We don't all have basements, but we know to get into the most interior room of the house, or building, and take cover. I've seen a few tornados from a distance, and have taken cover when under tornado warnings, but thankfully, my house has never been hit. We did experience baseball sized hail this year during one of the storms, though. Usually by this point in the summer, the extreme weather has kind of dissipated, so now, we deal with major heat. The band director ensures we stay hydrated; we all have water bottles on the sidelines.

Right now we are practicing staying in step. Why do people have a hard time with that? It's seriously not that difficult. I would rather we start working on our routine, but Mr. Cunningham is forcing us to march back and forth over and over until everyone gets in step. At least Aaron isn't missing anything fun, since he isn't here. Our practice is two hours long, and everyone is flushed and sweaty by the time we are finished. We will have to get used to marching in the heat again.

I notice towards the end of our practice that some of the football boys are sitting in the stands. They must have two-a-days practice after we finish on the field. All of a sudden, my heart starts beating really fast when I see Aaron's red truck turning in to park behind the stands by the field house. I hurry over to his truck to try and talk to him before he goes in, but it's too far and I can't get there fast enough. I see him get out and go inside. I decide to write him a note and leave it on his truck under the windshield wiper. I don't want to seem desperate, but he owes me an explanation at least. I won't give up on him, or us, until I know what is going on.

> Aaron,
>
> I have been trying to text you and I've left several messages on your voicemail. I saw that your Facebook page is inactive too. What is going on? Are you ok? I miss you. Please contact me and let me know you are alright.
>
> Love,
>
> Mia

I leave the note without anyone noticing because the team hasn't come out yet. I hope nobody messes with it. I guess if I don't hear from him, I will see him at school. I'm just relieved to see that he is at football practice. I was starting to wonder if I would ever see him again.

On Tuesday, Mr. Cunningham starts teaching us a routine. It's a little cooler tonight, but still in the 90's. I am hopeful that I will see Aaron again tonight. I don't know what their schedule is like, but I keep watching to see if the football kids are showing up when our practice is almost over. When I notice a few boys arrive behind the stands, I anxiously watch for Aaron's truck again, hoping I can catch him before he goes in to suit up. Mr. Cunningham tells me to pay attention because everyone is moving around me and I am standing in one spot, like a big dork. Oops. I feel embarrassed, but my emotion quickly changes when I see Aaron driving towards the field. I can't stop watching him until he gets parked. Mr. Cunningham is still talking to the band and hasn't dismissed us yet, and I'm fidgeting around, dying to just run to Aaron and talk to him. When we are finally free to go, I run to where Aaron's truck is parked, and he's gone again. I feel so sad and frustrated. I parked behind the stands today because I was hoping to see Aaron; however, since I've missed him yet again, I walk to my car with my head down in disappointment.

Right as I open my door, I hear, "Mia." It's Aaron. I look back and see him coming out of the field house, looking so incredibly handsome in his football uniform. Somehow, he looks taller and bigger with his pads and everything on. He walks toward me, looking like he's trying to hurry. I stand there, paralyzed, waiting to see what he's going to say. He isn't smiling. He just looks like he's determined and on a mission or something. It feels like it is happening in slow motion. Aaron reaches my car and comes around to where I'm standing, still holding onto my door.

"I can't talk long. I am supposed to be inside, and it won't be long until coach notices I'm not there."

"Ok. Well, did you get my note that I left on your truck last night?"

"Yes, I got it. I'm sorry I haven't been able to see you or talk to you. My parents have turned into over-protective freaks; they took my phone and disabled my Facebook account. I haven't been allowed to go anywhere by myself. It has really sucked," Aaron explains.

"So, you weren't ignoring me because you were mad at me or anything like that?"

"No, of course not, but I figure you won't want to be with me anymore since I will never get to see you. My whole family is crazy. I don't want you to have to deal with that," he says.

"I'm pretty sure I knew what I was getting into when I first started dating you, Aaron."

He looks down, "Maybe, but the situation has changed. My bio mom is looking for me, and if she finds me, I don't want you to be involved."

"I want to be involved, though."

"I don't know what she is capable of, especially if she is hanging around my dad again, Mia. I can't be responsible for something bad happening to you. I care about you, but I think we need to break up. Things are just crappy right now. I'm sorry."

Before I could say anything, the coach yells out the door, "Alexander, get your butt back in here, NOW!"

Aaron looks at me, sadly, one last time, before turning to run back in.

I sit down in my car, in disbelief, and start to cry.

~~~~~~~~

It's Saturday, and Mom is taking Lily and me to the mall to buy a few more back to school things. I hope it will get my mind off of Aaron. Lily and I are built completely differently. Lily is tall and skinny with a cute figure. She is very pretty and has dark, blonde hair. It seems like everything fits her well. I, on the other hand, am relatively short and very curvy, so I have to try on lots of different outfits to find what flatters me the most. Since Lily has already bought everything she needs, she and mom have their arms full of things for me to try in the dressing room. We choose one of the biggest dressing rooms so we can all fit in it. I definitely prefer for mom and Lily to be able to help me choose my outfits without me having to go out of the dressing room to show them. Plus, as I take off the clothes, I hand them to mom and she hangs them back on the hangers. We always laugh at the clothes that look ridiculous, as I flaunt them in the mirror and act like they are actually cute. However, at the moment, I'm feeling frustrated, because I am very indecisive today. I want each outfit to be perfect. I want to look good on the first day back to school, but I know that I really just want Aaron to notice me and think I look cute. I don't know if it's because I want him to regret breaking up with me, or I want him to immediately want me back. I just need to look good. After trying on a million different things, and creating "maybe," "definitely not," and "definitely yes" piles, we all discuss and decide on the top four outfits. Now I just have to figure out which one to wear tomorrow.

Lily and I also got some new shoes to complete our outfits, as well as a few miscellaneous accessories. We already got the school supplies we need the other day, so we are ready for school, at least physically. I don't know if I'm ready for school mentally, though. I am so nervous. I've always been nervous on the first day back, but this year, I feel extremely stressed. I want to see Aaron, but I don't want to see him, all at the same time. *God, please let tomorrow, and my whole junior year, be great, no matter what happens. In Jesus' Name, Amen.*

~~~~~~~

I called Carla last night, and we agreed to meet in the student parking lot so that we can go in to school together. I know it will help my confidence if my best friend is by my side. I am excited to be able to drive my car to school for the first time, and I proudly park it in the lot, not too far from the door. Lily gets out and heads in so she can find her friends. I see Carla waiting for me outside, so I get out of my car, thinking now or never. We walk in, and I keep my head up and smile, greeting various students who are already in the halls as we walk to the gym. I feel determined to have a good first day back to school. Some of the students have been going to this school for a long time. I think there are seven kids in my class who have gone to school together every single year since our very first day of kindergarten. It's weird because having been classmates for so long doesn't take away my nervousness. I don't want to necessarily be like the popular girls, but I want people to like me.

In the gym, Carla and I sit up in the top corner of the bleachers, and notice the changes in all of our friends that happened over the summer.

"Holy cow, look at Josh. He has facial hair. He looks way older than us," Carla comments.

"Seriously. That's crazy! And I think Caleb is like a foot taller. How can people change so much in just a few months?"

"Well, it seems like it's mostly the boys who have changed more. I mean, I feel like we look older, but the guys look like they are taller and more built," Carla continues.

"I'm scared to see Aaron. I've been trying not to think about it, but just seeing everybody is making me think about all of the changes we went through together over the summer."

"I understand. I'm really sorry, Mia. Maybe he will quit being weird and get back with you. I don't understand why y'all broke up anyway."

"He said he couldn't be with me because he is so busy with school and football and everything," I say, omitting the main reason for our break-up.

"Whatever. We're all busy. Maybe I should ask him what his deal is or get Jamie to talk to him."

"It's ok. Just leave it alone. I'm just going to try to not worry about it, and maybe eventually Aaron and I can at least be friends again," I say, trying to reassure myself more than anyone.

As if on cue, Aaron walks into the gym and immediately finds my eyes before looking away and joining some of the other football guys who are cutting up and acting crazy. My heart beats faster, and I wonder if I will really ever be able to just see him as a friend again. He means so much to me, and I hate this weird barrier in between us now.

The bell rings, and we all head to our home rooms to get our schedules for the year. Our home room is listed on a roster on the wall outside of the gym, so everyone knows where to go. All of my classes are easy today, although a little boring. In each class, the teacher explains the rules for the class and tells us what to expect for the year. I think most of my classes are going to go well this year, and I like all of my teachers, except for one. Mrs. Carper is not only strict, but she assigns a ton of homework in algebra 2. She is really old, and I think if she could hit students' hands with rulers, she would. She is old-fashioned and mean. I've always been a good student, but I don't know if I can be good enough for her, and from what I hear, everyone gets in trouble in her class at least sometimes. Today, she gave us a list of rules for her class that are a page and a half long. Carla and I joked about the stupid rules when we left for lunch.

"We can't wear clothes that match. We can't breathe. We can't look at each other," we joked, as her rules are THAT crazy!

Carla and I went to lunch at my house. We only have thirty minutes so even though I don't live too far from the school, by the time we take off driving time, we have around fifteen whole minutes to eat. I'm not complaining, though. Pretty much anything we think of making at my house will be better than our cafeteria food. Today, we made ourselves cheese burritos, which consists of cheddar cheese melted inside a flour tortilla and rolled like a burrito. When dipped in salsa, it's pretty darn good. The other good thing about going to my house is that I don't have to worry about seeing Aaron in the lunchroom. I am trying to avoid him as much as I can for right now because it hurts too much to see him. He looks sad, and I hate that. Band class is last period again, and avoiding him in that class is difficult.

Now school is over and I'm waiting for Lily to meet me at my car so we can go home. I made it through my first day back without anything horrible happening, and I'm ready to hurry and get home before anything can change that. *Lily is taking forever; she's so going to get it if she doesn't hurry and get in my car.* While sitting in my car, seemingly safe behind my tinted windows, I watch all of the football kids walking over to the field for after-school practice. I see Aaron, and I can't help but just stare at him. I watch as he walks alone, instead of with the other guys. I want to talk to him so badly; it's killing me. I decide I'm torturing myself by looking at him, so I look down at my phone and hit the Facebook app. While waiting for it to load, I look up just in time to see Aaron is outside my window just about to knock on it. His fist stops mid-air when he sees me look at him so instead, he gestures for me to roll down the window, so I do.

"Mia, you're killing me by staring at me like that."

"I wasn't staring at you. What are you talking about?" I lie, thinking surely he didn't see me.

"Ummm, yeah, you were. I can still see you even though your windows are tinted."

He shakes his head and looks right into my eyes, "This is hard for me too you know. Do you think I like having to give you up because my stupid past is still haunting me? We are just going to have to get used to this, though. I can't be who you need. Please understand that. I know it's early, but I would still like to be friends if you think that's possible. I miss being able to talk to you."

Is he trying to make me cry? I just want to get out and hug him, but I know that it's not a good idea.

"I want to stay friends, too, Aaron. It's just hard. Give me some time. Oh, and I will TRY not to stare at you, ya big egomaniac," I say smiling, trying to relieve some of the tension.

Aaron smiles back, "Thank you, Mia. I'll see you around." He turns and jogs to the stadium, and I see Lily coming out of the school. *It's about freaking time!*

Chapter 6
September

It's Friday, and we have been going to school for two weeks. Aaron and I have had minimal conversations, but nothing too awkward. Tonight is our first football game, and we are in the band hall getting ready to march to the stadium. I hate my uniform, and the hat is ridiculous. Our band hasn't had new uniforms in many years. People always alter the pants, so the sizes aren't accurate. We have to try on a million pairs before finding some that are probably still high-waters and have bulging pockets. It's either that, or get some that have a crotch that hangs down about two inches too far. The hats are pretty awful, too, and they mess up my hair. We have to wear them to and from the stadium, as well as on the field during half-time, but that leaves the whole time in the stands for me to have hat hair. I try not to think about that as we line up to march over. We get lined up, slowly but surely, and start to march to our drum cadence. I have to admit that even I have a little trouble staying in step with this cadence, considering it's not very together.

We finally take our places in the stands in time to play the school song and then the fight song, as everyone cheers for the players running through the big "Pluck the Eagles" poster onto the field. The announcer in the press box is the same guy who has done it for the past ten years I think. He calls for a moment of silence since we aren't allowed to pray, even though most of this town consists of church-going people.

Following the semi-silent moment among a large and excited crowd, the refs call the team captains to the center of the field to flip a coin. I see Aaron suited up on the sideline, wearing number fifty-one. *He looks hot.* We play six-man football in Coyote since we are such a small school. There are probably around fifteen to twenty kids on the sidelines, and Aaron runs out for the first play after kick-off. He is a receiver, and after several drives, the quarterback throws a long pass to Aaron, and he runs it in for a touchdown. The crowd is ecstatic, and roars with applause. Football is a huge deal in West Texas, and in our small town, football and basketball are the main sports. We won about half of our games last year, so to get a touchdown right at the beginning of the game makes us all hopeful for a better year this year. I am happy that Aaron is doing so well.

I notice that some of the cheerleaders are yelling for him specifically, and I can't help but feel jealous. I don't even know if he can hear them, but I feel angry that they are trying to steal my boyfriend who isn't really my boyfriend anymore. They may not even know we dated during the summer. I still hate it, though.

Our half-time went ok, considering we got through it without anyone getting hurt. We have been working on this routine for three weeks, but it's not quite enough to be great yet. However, the second half of the game is even better than the first. The score at half-time was 42-7 with us on top. We only need two more touchdowns or one touchdown plus a field goal to 45 the other team. In six-man football, when one team scores 45 more points than the other, the game is over. The opposing team, the Eagles, score right away, making our win by 45 points a little more effort, but the Coyote Hunters immediately answer with a touchdown on the kick-off return. The Eagles are unable to score again, and our team scores the second touchdown needed to 45 the other team, with thirty seconds remaining in the third quarter. Our crowd is jumping up and down with enthusiasm, high-fiving each other and looking forward to a great year, considerably different than anything we have seen in a long time. The team has Aaron lifted up on their shoulders as they celebrate their first victory. I can see the Alexanders in the stands cheering and clapping along with everyone, and I wonder if they realize how much their son has contributed to the first big win Coyote has had in a long time.

~~~~~~~

In the gym Monday morning, I notice that everyone is flocking to Aaron after his Friday night debut as the new football star of Coyote. He looks humble and a little embarrassed, especially when several of the cheerleaders sit by him and practically throw themselves at him. I hope this blows over because it's driving me insane watching everyone try to be his new best friend when they don't even know him. It makes sense that he is more popular after he did so well at the game, but he's still the same Aaron. I know him better than everyone else, and I can't even really talk to him about everything except to tell him he did a great job. Anything else would cross the line for us.

The entire week is like this, all of the students hanging all over Aaron, and everyone is excited to see him play again tonight against the Basin Bobcats. It is another home game tonight, and the stands are even more packed than last week. There are even people standing along the fence to watch the big game. I see quite a few people who have graduated within the last several years, all congregating with each other to watch this year's team perform. My parents are always at the games to watch the band, and I notice my mom is sitting next to Kathleen Alexander. I wonder if they are talking about anything other than the game. The players are on fire at the start of the game, and they score two touchdowns in the first half to the Bobcats' zero.

We march onto the field for our half-time routine, and it is remarkably better than last week. I think the excitement for the football program has motivated everyone to try harder to perform at the best of his or her abilities. I feel the energy from the crowd as they applaud, and I smile with pride for my school, our team, and for our band, before marching back to our spots in the stands.

In the third quarter of the game, we are initially playing defense. Aaron is the corner, and he catches an interception and runs fifty yards for a touchdown. The crowd goes wild as Aaron comes to the sidelines to rest for a minute, the coach congratulating him by smacking the back of Aaron's helmet. The Bobcats come back with two touchdowns within the third quarter, apparently having regained their desire to win, which puts us only one touchdown ahead for the last quarter of the game. The cheerleaders lead the crowd in motivated cheers, and everyone is stomping in the stands, creating a thunderous sound that can probably be heard for miles. The players hit each other, all getting pumped up and excited, and they stop any future scores of the Bobcats. We score two more touchdowns in the last five minutes of the game, and once again, annihilate our opponents.

Mom said I could hang out at the pumps for a little while after the game because everyone will be there celebrating together. She told me to be extra careful, especially considering there may be a lot of people drinking, and of course, I assure her I will be cautious. Carla and Jamie come with me, and we hang around all of our friends, talking and being silly since everyone is in a fun mood after the game. Aaron is not here, which seems unfair to him, considering he just played such an awesome game. I really hope the Alexanders will loosen up their tight rein on him. I can't wait to ask mom about her sitting by Kathleen. I was hoping mom could tell Kathleen that this is a safe town, encouraging her to chill out.

~~~~~~~

Today is Sunday, and I'm so thankful for my church. It is so nice to always have a constant in my life, a place where I can go to praise God and learn about Him. I've been so stressed out, and I forget to give it all to God like I'm supposed to. Today's lesson was actually about not being anxious, and trusting God. I know that I haven't done a great job of that lately, so I pray for God to forgive me and help me to do better. After church, my family went out to eat lunch like we frequently do, and then I took a nap after I practiced my flute for a while.

Entering the side doors close to where our youth meets, I see Kathy and Ken getting stuff ready for tonight. I am there early hoping for a chance to talk to Kathy for a minute, so she takes me to her office.

"How has school been going? The last I talked to you, you said Aaron had a lot of people talking to him after he did well in football."

"Well, he had a great game again on Friday. Mom sat next to his mom, and she said Kathleen, Aaron's mom, told her that she has to protect Aaron because his bio mom contacted Kathleen on Facebook and told her that Aaron is not Kathleen's kid, but hers (his bio mom). She said she wasn't going to let him go just because the court said she has to, and that Aaron used to sell drugs with his dad and that he stole things and that she needs him back to help her," I tell her.

"Do you believe he really did those things? Would it matter if he did, assuming he isn't doing it anymore?" Kathy asks me.

"I really don't think he would have done that stuff. Aaron talked about his bio parents doing that, but he sounded like it bothers him. Mom said she told Kathleen that maybe the bio mom was just trying to make her think badly of Aaron so that she wouldn't want him anymore."

"Did Kathleen agree with that thought?"

"I think she told mom that she thought that, too, but that either way, she loves Aaron, and is worried about the bio parents doing something crazy to get him. I guess that is why they have been so protective. I don't know what to think. I feel like our town is safe and that they should let him be a teenager, but I guess my opinion doesn't really matter," I say, feeling down.

"I really wish y'all could get them to come to church so Ken could meet them. I think he could help them a lot. Every situation is different, but his insight would probably be helpful and encouraging to them. Why don't you try asking Aaron again, and maybe your mom could also invite Kathleen? For now, we will continue to pray. Let's pray together before everyone gets here:

> *Father God, I lift up the Alexander family to You and ask for Your protection over them, as well as wisdom, strength, and encouragement. Help them to trust in You, and if they don't already have a church home, please direct them here. Please give Mia and her family the right words to say to them, Your words. Also Lord, please help Aaron's bio parents to find You and to turn from the sins with which they are struggling. Help them to see Your love, so that they can know that Aaron is where he should be. In Jesus' Name, Amen."*

"Amen. Thank you Kathy. You always know the perfect things to say to make me feel better," I tell her.

"Actually, Mia, God gives me those words. I pray for myself to have the right words too. Just say a silent prayer before you talk to Aaron next time," Kathy says.

I tell her that I will definitely do that, and I have more peace than I have had in a while.

Chapter 7
October

September went by quickly, and the fall weather in October is providing some really nice evenings for marching and for football. I haven't really had much time to talk to Aaron this week, but I told him that after the last game, which was away, we saw that they talked about Aaron and the Coyote Hunters on the 10:00 news. The sports guy was saying that Aaron has a lot of potential and that he has lead our team to some great wins so far. Apparently, the news people are sending a crew out to Coyote tonight to cover the game. It is homecoming, and everyone has been wearing big mums and garters at school today, creating an atmosphere filled with little bells ringing and lots of school spirit. I have a feeling this will be the largest homecoming game ever.

We are sitting in the section marked for the band during the pep rally. The cheerleaders are having all of the grade levels compete to see who has the most spirit. They direct each grade to yell, "We've got spirit, yes we do, we've got spirit, how 'bout you?" This week, the 5th graders are extremely loud, so they win the "spirit stick" until next week, which means they will have the decorated stick in their classrooms for the week. The elementary kids really get into it, but the high school students tend to be a little less enthusiastic. They are too cool to make a scene. The band has a list of songs to play, and the football players are set up in a section on the basketball gym floor, all wearing their football jerseys, as they always do on Fridays. The pep squad is doing a skit where some of the football players are dressed up like cheerleaders and some of the cheerleaders are dressed up like football players. They picked some of the biggest guys to do the skit, so it's pretty funny as they do cheers. Josh really looks funny dressed as a cheerleader since he has a beard.

The homecoming court is sitting together in the middle of the gym. They will be all dressed up tonight during half-time, and a fancy convertible car will parade them around the track that surrounds the field. It never fails that the homecoming court consists of the popular kids. Aaron has apparently made that list because he's one of the three guys. The girls are paired up with the guys, making a total of three couples. It bugs me to see Kelly sitting with Aaron. It looks like she thinks this gives her the right to claim him as hers or something. I think the homecoming court is a stupid popularity contest and an unnecessary part of the tradition of homecoming, but obviously that's partly because I'm not on it, even though I would never admit that to anyone.

The pep rally is at the end of the school day, so now that it is over, we head to the band hall to get ready for the game. We will go to the field early because the band parents are feeding us box suppers tonight, and we will eat in the stands before we have to play the pre-game songs. People are getting to the field early in order to get good seats knowing the stadium will for sure fill up for tonight's game.

The football boosters always sit together in the middle of the stands. They all have cowbells that they ring throughout the night, and I'm super thankful that I don't have to sit near them. I know they are excited, but the cowbells drive me nuts. Plus, some of them get way too vocal if the refs make a mistake. There is one dad who yells at his son constantly and a couple of other dads who are almost as bad. I always feel a bit sorry for those players. They are good players, but they seem to be under a lot of pressure, and I am more of a mindset that it's just a game. Plus, it would be embarrassing to have your parent constantly screaming at you from the stands. Aaron's parents are clearly proud of him, but they are much less vocal. They weren't raised in this city, though, where football is so emphasized.

Our team has always tried to arrange homecoming to be against a school who has a less competitive team so that we would have a chance to actually win. This year, ironically, the other team is doing quite well. They are undefeated just like we are. There are quite a few people in the visitors' stands too because we are playing against a small town that is only about thirty miles from us. Their mascot is the Prairie Dog, which I think is pretty lame. I always wonder why schools choose mascots that don't portray bravery or fighting skills. I mean, really, who the heck is going to be scared of a prairie dog? They might as well have picked a marshmallow to be their mascot. Our mascot is kind of dorky, though, so I guess I shouldn't be too critical. I think being the Hunters makes us sound somewhat tough, but the costume looks like a man with a big cowboy hat, boots, and a gun. He has a big handle-bar moustache and huge features on his big head. He sort of looks like a bobble head. The guy who wears the costume does a good job, though. He's really funny, and he's also good at interacting with the fans.

The game is really close the whole time, and in the fourth quarter, we are actually tied. With thirty seconds left in the game, the other team has possession, and they are trying to throw a long pass so they can score and win. Their quarterback throws the ball long, and it seems like it is in slow motion, heading straight for the intended receiver, when Aaron jumps up and snags the ball with one hand at the last second. He takes off running and makes it to our twenty before he is tackled. There are fifteen seconds left on the clock, and the crowd is practically going nuts as the coach directs the team to go for the touchdown instead of attempting a field goal since our kicker hurt his ankle earlier in the game. The first play is a running play, and we are stopped with five yards to the goal. The mood is tense. Then, the quarterback fakes a pass right, and follows with a pass straight to Aaron, who is already waiting in the end zone. We score with two seconds left on the clock. Our backup kicker kicks the extra point, which is good, and we remain undefeated. The camera crew has been at the game the entire time, filming different things. It was too close for them to leave, and both teams have been recognized lately since neither have been as good in the past. Our team huddles up in the middle of the field, and as we play the fight song, the crowd stays in the stands, clapping along, as everyone is elated.

After the game, Carla and Jamie and I hang out at the pumps. Everyone there is fired up from the game, and there are a ton of people there since a bunch of ex-students were here for the game. I see Aaron drive up and park, and I am shocked as he gets out and says he can hang out with us for a while. In my excitement to see him, I hug him, before I remember we are not a couple. He actually hugs me back, though, and I feel so overwhelmingly happy to be near him again, in his arms.

"Great game!" I tell him, smiling.

"Thanks," he says, kind of shyly.

Before we can say anything else, a huge group of people comes up, and everyone is patting him on the back and telling him how awesome the end of the game was. I move to the side and just watch as he receives credit for his amazing winning catch. Carla and Jamie stand beside me, and we are talking among ourselves, even though there is a mob of people next to us with Aaron. We aren't normally part of a popular group, and we feel more comfortable out of the spotlight. After maybe ten minutes of that, though, Aaron walks back over to us.

"Let's go get some ice cream. I need to get out of here. I feel like I'm being suffocated," he grins, enjoying the attention, but not for too long.

"Sounds like a great idea, man. We haven't done this in forever," Jamie says.

Carla just got a new car, a big, double cab truck, so we all hop in, Aaron and me in the back.

"This is different. I kind of like not having to be the one to drive, for a change," I say.

Carla has a CD playing, and I realize right before the song comes on, that she's playing this CD for a reason. I've been dwelling on my break-up with Aaron, and I listen to this song when feeling down and sorry for myself. Carla knows the song, "I Won't Give Up," by Jason Mraz is my song to Aaron, and I'm totally going to kill her if he figures out what she's doing. I feel myself blush as it plays.

"So..." I say, trying to cover up my face burning. I just know it is obvious that this song means something to me. "How does it feel to be the big football star?" I ask Aaron.

He smiles at me, "I don't want to talk about it. I like this song, too." *Dang it. How does he always know when I'm hiding something?*

I change the subject again, determined to not give in, "It was pretty cool to have the news people at the game."

"Not as cool as this song," he says, smirking at me.

"Ugh. You better stop teasing me," I say, smacking him on the arm playfully, but he grabs my hand and holds it, still looking at me.

"Aaron, I don't know if this is a good idea. I've had to try really hard to be 'just' friends with you, and I can't handle it if you blur the lines."

"Mia, I am so sick of always living in fear, always putting my life on hold while I wait for things to get better. I am still worried about your being involved with me because of my past and the threat I'm dealing with right now, but I hate being apart from you. I miss you so much."

Is this real? I better not wake up tomorrow to realize it was just a dream. That would just suck. I smile at Aaron, and think about how my last thought is such an understatement.

"What are you smiling at? You're making me nervous that I'm making a fool of myself. Do you still even like me for more than a friend?" Aaron asks, self-consciously.

I giggle, "I do still like you." My "funeral smile" is getting the best of me. I hate it when I smile or laugh at inappropriate times, but I really just feel happy. The thought of him being self-conscious shouldn't make me laugh, but I can't help it.

"Thanks for laughing at me, Mia. You are really boosting my confidence here," Aaron says, smiling in return because it's infectious.

"I'm not laughing at you. I promise. I'm just happy to be here with you right now. Seriously," I say, trying to convince him.

"Ok, ok. I believe you. Now scoot over closer to me. You are way too far over there in this huge truck."

I scoot over when Carla stops at a light, since I have a chance to get re-buckled. Aaron yells up to the front, "You're truck is a little big, don't ya think Carla? Is that to make up for being short?" We all laugh because she really is tiny in this giant truck. She loves it, though, so she doesn't care.

We are in a different town this time because we decide to go the opposite direction from Coyote. Llano is smaller, but there is a Dairy Queen that is still open since it's Friday night, and they have good ice cream. We all pile out of the car and go inside to order. I get a hot fudge sundae, my favorite, and after the others get their ice cream, we sit outside at the little tables near the play area. There aren't any little kids here this late, so we have the place to ourselves at the moment. My sundae is so delicious. Aaron got a brownie blizzard and we give each other a taste. His is good too, but not as good as mine. We sit there, just talking and hanging out, until a big group of teenagers gets there and kind of takes over the place. They are rowdy, playing on the play equipment, and acting obnoxious. We decide to leave, but we each get a drink to go before heading back to Coyote.

On the way home, I feel nervous because I'm determined to invite Aaron to church again. I really hope this time he will come. Thankfully, Carla stops trying to embarrass me with her song choices, and the radio is playing quietly. I remember Kathy's suggestion to say a silent prayer first, so I pray in my head.

> *God, please give me Your words and help me to invite Aaron to church. Please also help him to be receptive. Thank You God. In Jesus' name I pray, Amen.*

"Aaron, have you thought anymore about coming to church with me? I really want you, and your family, to come with us on Sunday, and then you could come with me to youth in the evening. Please, please, please?" I ask sweetly, with puppy dog eyes, as I try to lighten the mood but still show him how much I want him to come.

"Let me talk to my parents about it tomorrow, and I will try to call you, Ok? I have my phone back now."

"Awesome! I hope they will say yes! Yay!" I'm just a little over-excited and hopeful.

Aaron smiles at me, "Excited much?"

"Yes, I am, thank you very much."

He laughs and puts his arm around me for the rest of the ride home. *I know I'm only 16, but I really think I'm in love with this boy.*

~~~~~~~~

I told my mom about last night. She was happy for me that I'm back together with Aaron, mainly because she knows I'm happy. She said maybe I'll finally quit moping around all the time. I also told her about asking Aaron to go to church with us, and she decided to call Kathleen and ask her as well. Mom said Kathleen mentioned not having a church home at the game when they were sitting together, but they got distracted by Aaron making a touchdown and didn't get back to their previous conversation regarding church. I feel very encouraged by this as I sit in the kitchen with mom when she calls.

Mom greets Kathleen, "Hi. This is Sylvia. How are you?"…"We're doing well. So, have you talked to Aaron today?"…"Yes, Mia told me. She's very happy, which makes us happy too."…"Well, that's what I was calling about. Mia told me she asked Aaron to come to church with us, and since you and I talked about church a little a while back, I wanted to talk to you and see if you have any questions."…"Yes, it is non-denominational and pretty laid back. Oh, and people dress more casually."…"Great. We look forward to seeing y'all in the morning. It starts at 10:00, and we will meet you in the foyer so we can find a spot to sit together."…"Ok, see you tomorrow. Bye."

"That sounds like it's a yes," I say, waiting for mom to confirm what I'm thinking. She nods and says they are coming. I am overjoyed!

~~~~~~~~

We get to church a little early this morning, which is unusual for us because Lily and I tend to take too long getting ready which makes us late half the time. It was easy to get up this morning, though, knowing Aaron would be at church. We always park in the back of the church which is closest to the sanctuary, but there is a visitor lot in the front of the building, so I have a feeling the Alexanders will park there, which means they will come through the doors closer to the youth and kids' classrooms. I decide to walk down to that side of the church to see if they are here yet. Before I can get all the way to the doors, I see them come in, and Aaron catches my eyes and smiles at me. I walk a little faster so I can greet them and show them where the rest of my family is. Ken is standing near the youth room, so I pull Aaron and his parents over to introduce them. Ken shakes their hands and greets Aaron, "Hey, dude! Glad you are here! You are coming back for youth tonight, right?"

"Yes; I'm coming with Mia," Aaron says, smiling.

"Awesome! I'll talk to you more then. Great to have y'all!" he says to the whole family, before I take them over to Mom and Dad.

After everyone says their hellos, we go into the sanctuary right as the music is starting. We are able to sit in our usual spot, which is the third pew in the middle section. There are two smaller sections on either side of us. A lot of the time, the youth sits together, but for today, Aaron and I sit with our parents. Eric and Emily went to their classes, and Lily is sitting with her friends.

There is a full band playing along with the worship leader, and there are backup singers on each side of him. It's pretty loud, and the congregation is clapping with the first song, "God's Not Dead (Like a Lion)" by the Newsboys followed by "O Praise Him" by David Crowder. Worship is my favorite part of church and I love to sing, but I'm not singing loud with Aaron standing next to me. He seems a little self-conscious, and I would be embarrassed for him to hear me anyway. His parents seem more at home. I wonder what kind of church background Aaron even has, if any. I kind of doubt his bio parents took him to church, and I would imagine the different foster homes probably had different beliefs from each other, too. He doesn't seem uncomfortable really, just maybe a little unsure.

We sing another three songs and then after a few announcements, the pastor walks up to the podium and preaches his sermon. Today, he is talking about God's love and grace for us. He says that God loves us no matter what we've done, who we are, the color of our skin, where we come from, that He loves us unconditionally. We just have to accept His love. He talks about how when we choose to accept Jesus as our Lord and Savior, the Holy Spirit will always be with us, helping us, and even though we will still make mistakes, we are covered by God's grace. We are supposed to repent and ask for forgiveness, but no matter what happens, God still loves us, and He always will. I can't help but wonder if Aaron is listening, if he already knows this, or if he is hearing it for the first time. I want Aaron to know that God loves him. I want him to have that peace, especially since he's been through so much.

At the end of the service, the trays are passed for communion. In our church, everyone takes communion, so when the plate is passed, I whisper to Aaron that he can take communion if he wants to. He picks up the little cracker, representing the body of Christ, and then the grape juice, which represents the blood of Christ. An elder of the church prays over it, and we take it together. After the worship team leads us in one more song, we are dismissed. *I really hope Aaron wasn't freaked out or anything. I hope he likes it here and that they will keep coming.*

"So...what did you think about our church?" I ask Aaron as we are walking towards the gym, where the youth hangs out until the parents are finished talking. The grown-ups can talk forever.

"It was ok, a little different from anything I've been to, but I thought it was fine."

"What kind of churches have you been to?"

"I've been to Catholic Church with a couple of my previous foster families, and then we went to a really small church with this family for a while, but it was still pretty different. There wasn't a band and it was a lot quieter," he says, grinning.

"Yeah, our worship is pretty loud, but I like that part."

"I actually liked it, too," he says. "I think it was way better than anything I have seen in the other churches. I liked how people seemed happy, and everyone seems pretty normal here."

"That's good," I say, not knowing what else to really add to that. I hope when he comes to youth tonight that it will be even better. Youth is way more fun and everyone is cool there.

Our parents find us after about ten minutes of us hanging out in the gym, and mom tells me that the Alexanders are joining us for lunch. We are going to eat at a place that serves breakfast all day, along with other lunch foods. I love pancakes, so it sounds good to me. I ask if Aaron can ride with us to the restaurant, and his parents don't mind. *Yay!*

At lunch, our parents chat as if they have known each other forever. It sounds like the Alexanders like our church; Eric and Emily apparently enjoyed their classes, and I heard Kathleen tell my mom that that was an important factor for their choosing a home church. Aaron, Lily and I sit at the other end of the table, though, so I quit listening to our parents' conversation. We are taking turns stacking little coffee creamer things to see who can make the tallest tower. We have taken all of the ones from the little, metal holders in the middle of the table. Lily has managed to stack seven of them, which is the tallest, but then Aaron blows on it, causing it to fall, which makes us all crack up. Mom looks over just in time to see Lily getting back at Aaron by throwing a piece of egg that she didn't eat at him. It sticks to his cheek. Busted. Mom smiles and tells us to settle down.

"Yeah, Lily. Gosh!" I tease, giggling.

"Really, you need to set a better example for my younger siblings, Lily," Aarons adds, laughing.

"Shut up. Y'all started it. Buttheads!" Lily says back, grinning.

~~~~~~~

Aaron went home after lunch, but met me at my house so we can ride together back to Crockett for youth. Everyone is in the gym hanging out when we get there, so I introduce Aaron to a few of our friends. Some of the guys get him to shoot hoops with them, while Carla and I chat with the girls. When Ken comes in and yells for everyone to head to the youth room, Aaron rejoins me and Carla and we all walk together.

"We usually start with worship, sort of like we did earlier in church," I tell Aaron, knowing he's probably wondering what's next.

"Cool."

The music in youth is even louder and everyone dances, jumps, and puts their hands up. It's a lot more fun, sort of like a mini concert, with songs by bands like Skillet, Third Day, and Toby Mac. I kind of move to the music, but in a much more calm way because I don't want to make a fool out of myself, especially with Aaron there. He smiles at me, and kind of does what I do.

After worship, Ken divides the group into girls and boys, and then we split up into our own little groups of four or five. We each have an adult who leads our group, and we go to different parts of the church so we can have privacy. I like this part because I hate talking in front of a bunch of people. Ken and Kathy just started this several months ago, but our little group has gotten to know each other really well. Hopefully, Aaron will be put in a good group and will feel comfortable. I tell him I will see him later as Ken comes up to him to tell him where to go.

After about thirty minutes, the whole group gets back together, and Ken teaches a short lesson on the same topic we talked about in our small groups. Tonight, the topic is God's grace and forgiveness of our sins. We did an activity in our small groups where we wrote down our sins, things that we have problems with, and folded the piece of paper up. Back in the larger group, we are all holding our little folded pieces of paper. There is a big, wooden cross behind Ken, and he asks us to each come up, one by one, and tack our paper to the cross. While everyone is doing this, the room is quiet. Then Ken stands up again and says, "Jesus died on the cross. He took the punishment for all of our sins, and because of His sacrifice, our sins are washed away, and we are saved. No matter what you have done, God forgives you. You just have to ask for it. I want everyone in here to bow your heads as we pray together:

> Father God, Please help everyone in here to know You. Help us to understand your grace and help us to know that You love each and every one of us. Because You love us, You have sent Your Son to die on the cross. Father, please forgive our sins. We give it all to You, and we thank You for your love. In Jesus' Name we pray, Amen."

The whole youth echoes, "Amen."

"Alright guys, don't forget we are all going to the corn maize next weekend instead of coming here for youth. We will have pizza there so come hungry. See you next week," Ken dismisses us.

Carla, Aaron, and I get back in my car to go home after telling everyone, "bye." Ken shook Aaron's hand and told him he was glad Aaron came.

"Did you have fun tonight?" I ask Aaron, hoping it wasn't too much for him.

"I did. Ken is cool; I was in his small group."

"That's cool. I was hoping it wouldn't be uncomfortable for you in small groups since you don't know everyone yet."

"It wasn't bad. I didn't talk much, but I might after I get to know people better."

"I understand. It took me a while to talk, too," I say. "So, do you think you will keep coming?"

"If mom and dad are cool with it, I will."

"Yay. I'm so glad you liked it!"

He smiles, "There is another reason I like it."

"What's that?" I ask, just so I can hear him say it out loud.

"There's this super-hot girl who goes there too."

"Oh really?"

Carla chimes in from the back seat, "Thanks, Aaron. That's so sweet of you to call me super-hot, but Jamie might not like it very much." She laughs, which makes us laugh.

"Sorry Carla, but I only have eyes for one super-hot girl," he grins, looking at me.

"You better!" I tease him, feeling happy.

Since we have school tomorrow, Aaron leaves right when we get to my house, after giving me a kiss. It has been a great weekend!

~~~~~~~

This week at school has been interesting. The popular crowd seems a bit surprised that Aaron and I are back together. Some of them saw us together in the summer, but I guess they thought it was nothing. I can't help but feel a little like telling them all, "ha ha." They are so shallow and act like I'm not good enough to be with Aaron. It makes me angry. Aaron always tells me I'm beautiful and that they are crazy if they don't see it. He acts like he's proud to have me as his girlfriend, which even though I'm thankful about it, I don't get it. I guess I've always believed what the popular kids have told me that I wasn't as cute or cool as them. It bothers me that they don't like me. I don't really even see why; they don't even know me. I try not to think about it too much.

This week was also "Drug-Free" week, so each day, the school had a different activity. On Monday, we had "Wear Red Day," which was a good opportunity for me to wear my Texas Tech shirt. Aaron also had a Tech shirt on, so we kind of matched. The school passed out red ribbons that said, "Drugs are dumb," although mostly only the elementary and junior high kids wore them. Tuesday was "Wear a hat" day. The guys all liked this because they could wear hats to school. There were mostly baseball caps, and one guy wore a big sombrero, making everyone laugh. I wore my pink cowboy hat that I got when we went to the rodeo last year. Wednesday was crazy sock day, "Put a sock on drugs," but most of my socks are pretty normal, so I just wore non-matching socks. Aaron didn't participate that day. On Thursday, we were supposed to wear sunglasses for "Shade out drugs," but we couldn't keep them on during class, so it was kind of stupid.

Friday was the best, though, because the activity was "Say boo to drugs," and we were allowed to wear costumes since Sunday is Halloween. A whole bunch of people in our school wore costumes. Aaron, Jamie, and Carla, and I decided to dress up in an 80's rock star theme. I bought a crimping iron so Carla and I both crimped and ratted our hair to make it really big. I wore my Motely Crue shirt, and Carla wore her Bon Jovi shirt. We wore big hoop earrings and lots of makeup. Jamie and Aaron didn't tell us exactly what they were going to do to dress up because they wanted it to be a surprise, so we cracked up when we got to school and they had painted their faces like Kiss. They had black t-shirts and cut-up jeans. It was so funny. We didn't win the costume contest, but we thought we looked pretty cool.

The game Friday was away and the band didn't get to go because it was a two hour drive to our opponents. It bugged me to not watch Aaron play. We won, though, so Coyote is still undefeated.

~~~~~~~~

It's Sunday, and Carla invited Jamie to come to youth with all of us tonight. The Corn Maize is in a different small town than our church and is actually a little closer to where we live. We have to map it on my phone though because it's sort of out in the country. Aaron is happy to have Jamie with us this time. It would be really cool if we all went to the same church. Jamie's family already goes to a different church so he might not be able to come with us very often, but maybe he can come to youth.

At the Maize, we find our group of about twenty kids standing with Ken and Kathy. Ken tells us we are going to split into two big groups and see who can navigate the maze fastest. Luckily, we get to pick our groups, so Aaron, Jamie, Carla, and I are able to stick together. It's kind of creepy out here in the dark in a giant corn field, but we use our cell phone flashlights to help us see a little better. Our group enters first, and we are immediately surrounded by corn stalks that are probably about eight feet tall. It is pretty dense, and we can only see ahead of us, so when we reach a place where we can choose which direction to go, we all stop and look around, trying to figure out the best way. The group is not wanting to go the same direction, but Aaron suggests we take turns deciding. Everyone likes that idea, so we let him go first. He decides we will go right. When we get through a couple of other turns decided by different kids in the group, it's Carla's turn and she makes us go left. We all follow and end up in what we think is the same place, so since it's my turn next, I choose to go right. We finally make it to a sign that says we have made it half-way, and we have already been in the maze for 45 minutes. I'm starting to wonder if we will ever make it out. I'm starting to freak out a little, and I feel like I keep hearing weird sounds. Aaron is holding my hand, and we keep making our way, through the narrow halls formed by the corn stalks. When we finally reach the exit, we all cheer, and I think I might be happier than anyone to be out of there. I don't know who in the heck thought this would be fun, especially after scary movies have been made in corn fields. It took our team one hour and fifteen minutes. The other team started after we had been in the maze for thirty minutes. While they are still in there, we play various carnival type games. It is super crowded tonight since it's Halloween. I think that's partly why I was so scared in the maze. There are people dressed up in scary costumes, and I was terrified that one of them would jump out at us while we were in there. I'm pretty sure I would have passed out and they would have had to carry me the rest of the way out.

The other team made it out of the maze in one hour and five minutes. Their prize is to get to be first in line to get pizza. I don't consider that too big a loss. After we are all finished eating, we get to go on a hay ride. It's a big tractor pulling a long, flat-bed trailer with hay stacks lining the outside and also with a row on the inside. Aaron and I sit on the outside, enjoying the crisp air as we sit snuggled up close to each other. It is the best feeling to be in Aaron's arms. I love his smell, and I feel so protected with his arm around me.

"I love this," I tell him.

"The Corn Maize?" he asks.

"Ok, I didn't love the maze part, but I love being on this hayride with you."

"Me too. It's the best Halloween I've ever had."

"What did you do for Halloween while growing up?" I ask him.

"I think I went trick-or-treating a couple of times when I was little but mostly nothing."

"We always went trick-or-treating in Coyote since we knew everyone there. Plus, we always carved pumpkins when we were little," I add.

"I've never carved a pumpkin," he tells me.

"What? That's crazy. We will have to carve pumpkins for Thanksgiving or something since it's a little late to do it for Halloween. We could carve a turkey," I suggest.

"Cool. You can show me how."

"K. I'm no expert or anything though," I say, smiling.

"Really? That's the first thing I heard about you when I moved to Coyote: 'Mia is the expert pumpkin carver in this town.'" He said the last part with some kind of country sounding old man accent.

"Shut up. You're so crazy," I say giggling.

After the hay ride, it's already pretty late, and we head back home since we have school tomorrow. I think everyone had fun. I just hope I don't have scary dreams about that maze.

Chapter 8
November

It's the first Friday of November, and our last regular game before playoffs. Normally, this would be our last game of the year for Coyote, but since our team is kicking butt, who knows how long we will be in football season? It's a home game, and I think the whole freakin' town is here. The stands are packed, people are lining the fence, and some people are sitting in their cars parked around the end of the field. The visitor stands are not very full, but they did bring their cheerleaders and band. The news people are here again to highlight the Hunters. There are tons of little kids playing under the stands and running around, wearing beat tags to show their school spirit. The pep squad sells beat tags every game day morning at school. They are black or gold ribbons, and always say something corny, but the elementary kids love them and they wear them on their shirt. This week, since we are playing the Hornets, the beat tag says, "Take the sting out of the hornets!" There is an upside down, cartoon hornet with its legs in the air and the Hunter is chopping the stinger off. It's dorky, but it's tradition, which somehow makes it cool. Maybe it's just because when I was little, I loved getting a beat tag on Fridays.

It's pretty cold tonight, so people have blankets covering their laps in addition to coats and toboggans. Mr. Cunningham even lets the band students cover up with toboggans and blankets while we sit in the stands. I keep my hands under the blanket except for when we are playing because my fingers freeze when I hold my flute. It's too hard to play when I'm wearing gloves. Somehow, instead of making us miserable, though, the cold just adds to the excited atmosphere.

As usual, the band plays the fight song as the football players run through the poster that the cheerleaders hold at the end of the field. When I see Aaron, I realize it's the first game I get to watch him play as my boyfriend. Somehow all of my emotions for him are intensified as I watch him on that field. I feel pride that he's mine, excited for him, and nervous for him as well. *I think he's even more hot, too.*

After watching an intense first half, we watch the visitor's band perform on the field first while we wait on the side of the field. Their band is pretty good even though they are small. They play fun songs, all Michael Jackson hits. After they exit the field, we march on, ready to perform our last half-time for the season at home. We did this same routine the last home game, but we added a song for this show. We are playing songs from the Disney show, Aladdin. My part is really fun, so I love this show. The crowd is very supportive and loud when we finish, and I feel my adrenalin pumping as I realize I had been nervous to perform in front of such a huge crowd.

I smile as we march off the field, looking at the people standing by the fence in front of my yard line. All of a sudden, I notice one lady in particular, and she seems familiar. She's looking at me, and she isn't clapping like everyone else is. Then it hits me, it's her-- Aaron's bio mom. *Oh. My. Gosh!* She has a little smirk on her face, and I think she sees the recognition in my face. I look away, and we turn to march in front of the stands so we can play the fight song before taking our seats.

The second half of the game is crazy, each team scoring frequently, but we win by two touchdowns by the final buzzer. Our players are all jumping up and down on the field, and they pour ice water on the head coach. He laughs, even though he's got to be freezing since it's already really cold outside. I can't wait to see Aaron after the game so I can tell him who I saw.

~~~~~~~

I have to go to the band hall and change out of my uniform, but I hurry so I can meet Aaron as soon as he comes out of the field house. When he sees me waiting for him, he gets a huge smile on his face and comes and picks me up in a giant bear hug. His hair is all wet from taking a shower after the game, and he smells so good. *I could stay like this forever, wrapped in Aaron's arms. I love him so much.*

"Awesome game, babe!" I say, smiling back.

"Thanks, babe. It was crazy seeing so many people here for the game, huh?"

"Seriously! I've never seen it like that. I have to tell you something, though," I say, feeling worried again. He had momentarily taken my mind off of what I needed to tell him. I don't want to ruin his night or anything, but I have to do this.

"What's wrong? Is everything ok?" He can see my mood change.

"Everything's fine. I just...when we were finished with the half-time show, we were coming off the field, and I saw her by the fence."

"Who? Who did you see?"

"I'm pretty positive it was your bio mom. She was just standing there, and I think she recognized me because she was looking right at me, and she had kind of a weird smile on her face. What do you think we should do? How did she know you were here?"

"Crap." He looks away and kind of walks in circles while thinking.

"Are you sure it was her? I mean, you've only seen her a couple of times."

"I'm pretty sure, babe," I tell him.

"I wonder if my parents saw her. I don't have any missed calls or texts or anything on my phone. I think they would be blowing up my phone or even be here to make me come home if they knew."

"You're probably right. What should we do?"

"I'm not telling them. I mean, crap, Mia, we are finally getting to see each other more again, and I'm not going to let them freak out and keep me hostage in our house all the time anymore. I can handle my mom. She probably won't bother us anyway. She must have seen it on the news that I play here. I don't know how else she would know. Maybe she just wanted to see me play."

I really don't want anything to change for us either, especially after last time. I can't be apart from Aaron ever again. It sucked. It hurt. I hated it.

"Ok, I won't tell anyone, but if anything more weird or scary happens, I think we should tell someone. Ok?"

"We'll see. I'm not worried. Let's just forget about all of that and go celebrate. Come on," he leads me to his truck so we can find Carla and Jamie.

~~~~~~~

Aaron's family has gone to church with us several times now, and Thanksgiving is next week. Aaron's family is going out of town to visit his mom's parents for Thanksgiving. They will be gone for four days. Aaron said he isn't looking forward to it.

"I don't even know these people. I've met some of them once during the adoption at the courthouse, but I've never even met some of them. It's weird to be adopted. I'm not just adopted into my little family here but into a huge family of aunts and uncles and cousins and grandparents. In a way, it's cool to have a big family, but it's kind of hard to think of them as my family yet. Plus, they all hug me and crap, and my grandparents tell me they love me. I'm like, 'dude, I don't exactly know you.'"

"That would be weird I guess. They're nice at least, though, right?" I ask.

"Yeah, they're cool. It's just not what I want to be doing for the couple of days we have off of school. I would rather stay here."

"I know. I'm going to miss you!" I pout, and he leans in closer to me and gives me a kiss. We are laying on the trampoline in my backyard, after having eaten dinner at my house. Mom and Lily had gone to Crockett today, and they brought back pizza for supper. Living out in the country, I don't know what it's like to order pizza and have it delivered. We usually only eat out on the weekends, so it's a treat for us to have pizza tonight.

It's actually pretty warm today, even though it's November. You just never know what the weather will be like where we live. I never get used to how it can be hot one day and cold the next, no matter what month it is. I'm glad it's nice out, though, because I love being outside. One good thing, too, is that there aren't any bugs out right now; when the mosquitos are bad, it's horrible. Right now, we can hear the cows mooing in the field behind our house, which by the way, doesn't exactly sound like moo, but more like maaaa in a nasally voice.

There are hardly any trees around here, so we can see for miles, which might bug some people, but to me it is home. Aaron and I lie on our bellies facing behind my house, watching the cows that are silhouetted in the sunset. It feels romantic until we see my dog, Bo, chasing a rabbit. My dumb dog is so funny. He never catches one, but if sees a rabbit, he goes crazy and starts running after it, every single time. Aaron and I laugh as we watch Bo. Just then, Mom pokes her head out the back door and tells us to come in since it's getting dark. Plus, she made banana pudding, and I cannot resist that. Yum.

~~~~~~~~

Even though I really miss Aaron, I love Thanksgiving. My whole family goes to Grandma's and everyone brings certain foods, sort of like we did for 4th of July, but different kinds of food. Grandma always makes the turkey and dressing, which is good because I don't think anyone could make stuffing like she does. One of my aunts brings mashed potatoes and ham every year, one brings tea and dessert, and we always make green bean casserole, candied yams, and pumpkin pies. There is usually more than that, too. Everyone arrives at Grandma's around noon, and after Grandpa prays, we get our plates and get food so we can go sit at one of the three tables set up in three different rooms. I usually sit at the table in the den with my cousins.

After we eat, we always draw names for Christmas. Since our family is so big, we put everyone's name in a basket and pick one for whom we will buy a Christmas present. I reach my hand in the basket that my younger cousin is trying to hold up high so I can't see the names, and I pick one. It says, "Grandma." It won't be hard to pick out a present for her. I know how much she loves pictures, so maybe I will make a scrapbook of our family for her. Once all the names are drawn, some of the men watch football in the den, and the women and older kids sit at the kitchen table and play games. I love playing board games with my family. It is always so fun. We are playing a game called *Encore* and we have divided into two teams. Grandma is on a team with me and two of my cousins and we are playing against my mom, her sister, and another cousin.

Having Grandma on my team is like having a secret weapon in this game because she knows a ton of old songs. The team picks a card and picks one of the words on the card. Then each team has to think of a line from a song that has that word in it, and they have to sing the line. We don't play by the rules of the game, though. Instead, we just take turns going from one team to the other until we can't think of another song. The first word is "bad," so I sing, "You Give Love a Bad Name," by Bon Jovi. The other team comes back with the lyrics to "Bad to the Bone." Their whole team chimes in, "B-B-B-B-B-B-Bad, bad to the bone..." We all start laughing. My cousin on my team then sings another Bon Jovi hit, "Bad Medicine." My aunt on the opposite team sings a line from, "Bad" the Michael Jackson hit. Then Grandma sings, "I got it bad, and that ain't good." We all laugh, and she says, "What? It's an oldie but a goody." We think of around four more songs before moving to other words. We don't even care who won though because it is just fun to be together and act silly.

Later, Mom, Lily, and I go to Crockett at midnight to do Black Friday shopping, all wearing Christmas shirts. Mine is a long-sleeved black t-shirt that says, "Believe," written in glitter. We love getting good deals, and depending on what we are looking for, don't mind standing in crazy, long lines to get the cheap prices. We hit Target, Kohl's, the mall, one of the Christian stores, and a couple of other places. At Kohl's, the line is so long that we have to wait about an hour just to get to pay. Right when we get to the front, the lady in front of us passes out. It kind of freaks us out but she looks like she's ok. We haven't ever seen people fight over stuff like they show on the news every year, but some of the people do get pretty crazy when they are trying to get what they want. We always get so tired which makes us crack up at everything, but somehow, we shop all night long before driving back home to sleep. It's so fun. I love being out all night long.

Aaron texted me last night before we went shopping to tell me that their next play-off game is actually tonight, so I set my cell phone alarm to get me up at 2:00 so I will have time to get ready. The game is at a big stadium in Crockett, so Carla and Jamie are going to go with me to watch Aaron.

As Jamie, Carla, and I near the stadium, the streamers and signs decorating our side tell us where to park. We are playing on the home side, which is good because the sun isn't in our eyes while it's setting. The people sitting on the visitor side are all shading their eyes with their hands and they look uncomfortable. The only bad thing is that it is colder in the shade, especially as it gets darker. This stadium is really big; even with a bunch of people here from Coyote, it is still only half-full. There is a nice scoreboard that has a screen showing the game up-close. It's kind of cool to see Aaron on the big screen. Even though I love being in band, I'm enjoying not having to worry about it tonight so I can just watch the game, which really means, watch Aaron.

He looks so hot tonight. I watch him warming up on the sideline, and then he looks up into the stands. We are sitting pretty low, so I can see him smile and wink at me, making me blush. Sometimes, I feel like I'm dreaming because I don't think I will ever get used to having Aaron as my boyfriend. It feels too good to be true. I smile back at him and blow him a kiss. Jamie and Carla both laugh at me, making me feel like a dork, but I remind them that they do the same kind of stuff. "Y'all better shut-up," I say, laughing along with them.

Our team wins the coin toss and chooses to play offense first. We start strong and score on the first drive, daring the other team to just try to come back to that. Unfortunately, we are a little over-confident, and the other team immediately scores. The players on the other team are all celebrating and acting like we are going to lose. This looks like it's going to be a crazy game. The whole first half is intense, with both teams answering each other's scores, creating a very close game. At half-time, we are able to relax for a minute. I'm glad the visitor side is not connected to our side like in our home stadium. These crowds are rowdy and I'm afraid there would be more fighting than just on the field.

When the second half starts, both teams are hyped up and ready to finish with a win. This is the closest competition we have had this year. With five minutes left in the game, we are tied 35-35 and we have the ball. We are on our 40 yard line and making progress, when all of a sudden, our quarterback gets sacked, and he isn't getting up. The crowd is quiet, and the coaches and trainers run onto the field. The players on both teams are each kneeling on one knee as the various people tend to the injured player, Nick, a senior. Nick's dad walks out onto the field, and we are all very worried for our friend. Finally, we see him sit up, with assistance from the coaches, and they help him stand up and then walk slowly off the field, their arms under his arms. Everyone on both sides of the field claps, relieved to see he is able to walk off the field.

The game starts back, but with a different level of emotion. I think everyone still wants to win, but Nick's getting hurt changes everything. Our players are playing like they are angry, like they have to win for Nick if for no other reason. Our back-up quarterback is a sophomore, though, and he hasn't played this position in a game all year. He looks very nervous as he attempts a long pass to Aaron. The pass is way off, and Aaron has no chance of catching it. We get to the fourth down, and have to kick a field goal. Our crowd cheers, knowing the other team only has 2 minutes to try and score, hoping we have secured the win. We kick the ball to the other team, and they run it to the fifty yard line. They keep getting first downs until they are on their twenty yard line with 20 seconds left in the game. They are on their third down, and our entire crowd is on its feet, screaming, trying to help by distracting the other team. Their quarterback gets the ball, fakes a pass, and then runs it himself, for a touchdown, stunning the crowd on our side to silence, while causing the fans in the visitor stands to erupt with cheering. After kicking their extra point, the final score of the game is 42-38, officially ending our football season for this year. I can see the disappointment in all of our players' faces, as they walk with their heads down, to their huddle.

I hate it for Aaron, but I'm kind of thankful to be done with football for a while. I would never say that out loud, though. Football is everything to a lot of people around here. The whole team is quiet as they walk to the bus after the game, and Aaron doesn't look at me. I hope he's ok. We head back to Coyote, and I drive to the field house after dropping Carla and Jaimie off at her house. I'm hoping to see Aaron after he changes back into his regular clothes.

I stand leaning on the back of my Jeep Cherokee, arms folded across my chest because it's cold, and wait for Aaron to come out. When he does, he gives me a little smile, and comes to hug me. We hug for a long time, ignoring the other guys coming out telling us to get a room.

"Are you Ok? It was a great game, you know," I tell him.

"I'm fine. I wanted to win, but we didn't, so... I don't want to talk about it." Aaron kisses me, and I feel like I would fall if I weren't in his arms. *Yeah, I don't want to talk either.*

Aaron holds both of my hands and puts his forehead on mine. "Babe, I'm so glad I have you. Do you know that?"

"I think so, but I am MORE glad that I have you!" I say, teasing him.

"Not possible. You are so, so pretty, Mia. I missed you. Thank you for meeting me here; I don't think I could have waited until tomorrow to see you."

"I'm really glad you feel that way because that's exactly what I was thinking, and I was worried that you would be mad after the game."

"You mean more to me than that game, babe," Aaron says, reassuring me.

We stand there hugging for like five minutes before deciding it's way too cold to be outside.

"I'm freezing. You want to come to my house and hang out?" I ask him.

"Yeah. I need to let my parents know but I don't think they will care. They know I wanted to see you after the game." They text him back pretty quickly to let him know it's ok to come over, so he follows me in his truck.

He gets to hang out at my house for about an hour before his curfew, which gives us enough time to eat left-over turkey and stuffing that Mom brought home from Grandma's. I walk him to the door, excited that he said he will come back tomorrow. It's like I can't see him enough.

Chapter 9
December

I love Christmas time. I think it's my absolute favorite time of the year, and this year is the best ever since Aaron and I are together. I love being with him. He's so funny, and smart, and cute, and caring. *I love him!*

Aaron's parents finally let him reactivate his Facebook, so he checks his after I check mine on my laptop at my house. Aaron is over at my house for dinner, and we are sitting in the living room while sort of watching *Elf*. I've seen it a million times, so Aaron and I talk and play on the computer while still laughing at the funny parts of the show. Aaron cracks up when Buddy, the elf, chews the gum off of the rail, but my favorite part is when he is singing, "Baby, It's Cold Outside," with the girl in the bathroom.

Aaron signs onto his Facebook page, and there is a little red, number 1 on the message thing at the top of the page. I watch the movie, not paying attention to what Aaron is looking at, until I hear him say, "What the crap?"

I look at the screen sitting in Aaron's lap and see that the message is from Patricia, his bio mom. Aaron is staring at the screen, already having read what the message said, and waiting for me to read it too.

Aaron,

I watched your last two games. You're pretty good at football. I didn't know that. I was wondering if we could see each other since it is Christmas. I have a present I want to give you.

Your REAL Mom

"Wow," I say, not knowing what to think of this.

"I know," he says, quietly.

"You aren't really going to go see her, are you?" I feel worried about him. She is so creepy.

"I think I might. It's not like she is going to hurt me. What more can she really do to me? I can't believe she was at my last two games. You didn't see her at the last one, did you?"

"No; I would have told you if I had seen her. Aaron, what if she does hurt you? I'm scared for you to go see her. Don't you think you should tell your parents?" I am freaking out a little.

Mom walks by right as I say that, and says, "tell your parents what? Is everything ok?"

Aaron closes the laptop and smiles, "Everything is fine. We were just talking about Christmas presents."

Mom smiles back, "OK. It must be *some* present if y'all are being so secretive," as she walks back into the kitchen.

Aaron looks at me, "Babe, please don't tell anyone. I won't get hurt. I promise, and it would just upset my parents and make them worry."

I feel nervous about it, but I nod my head in agreement.

> *Lord, please protect Aaron and don't let him get into anything scary. Thank You. In Jesus' Name, Amen.*

We watch the rest of the movie and Aaron acts like nothing happened for the rest of the night. I hope he's right that nothing bad will happen. I can't stop wringing my hands, feeling worried, but when he leaves, Aaron reassures me and says everything will be fine.

~~~~~~~

It's Friday, and Aaron is driving my car with Jamie and Carla in the back, looking at Christmas lights. We drove to town because Coyote only has like 12 little streets, so there aren't many lights to see there. In Crockett, we are driving through some of the rich neighborhoods because they all have lights on their houses. It's really pretty, and I'm glad Aaron is driving so I am able to look at the lights. We've all grown close to each other, so we are having fun and are not embarrassed to be singing along with the Christmas music on the radio. After driving through several big neighborhoods, Aaron takes us to a place where little kids can visit Santa, and they sell hot chocolate. There are lights everywhere and little houses set up with decorations, sort of like a little Christmas village. We sit by a fire warming our hands while drinking hot chocolate. Then, we decide to get our pictures made with Santa. Carla and Jamie go first, and then Aaron and I both sit on Santa's lap for a picture together. We all laugh, even though I'm not sure Santa thought it was very funny. He still gives us each a little candy cane, and we all giggle as we walk back to the car.

After dropping Jamie and Carla off at Carla's house, Aaron drives us back to my house so he can get his truck.

"Thanks for driving tonight. I had so much fun," I tell him while holding his right hand since his left is on the steering wheel.

"I don't mind driving. It was fun, and I think I'm going to put my copy of our picture on the wall in my room," he says, laughing.

"It will make a good Christmas decoration for your room," I add, being silly.

When we arrive at my house, Aaron leaves the car running while we sit talking for a minute.

"Babe, I didn't really want to bring it up, but I know you will be mad at me if I don't. I'm going to visit my mom tomorrow night."

"What? Where are you meeting her?"

"At her house. She gave me the address. It's on the west side of town," he tells me.

"And you're sure you are safe doing this?"

"Yes. I'm not worried at all, and I'm kind of glad she contacted me. I know it's hard to understand, but she's my mom, and I miss her. Plus, she has sounded like things are better, so maybe she hasn't been drinking as much," he says, I think trying to reassure himself as much as me.

"Ok. Will you call me when you get home so that I know you are Ok? I want to hear about how it goes, too."

"Yes, I will call you. Since I won't see you tomorrow, I'm going to have to at least talk to you, ya know?"

I smile, "K. Please be careful, babe. Call me as soon as you get home!"

"I will. I promise."

Aaron gives me a kiss goodnight before he drives away.

~~~~~~~~

Luckily, Mom, Lily and I are Christmas shopping today. It helps pass the time until I hear from Aaron about meeting with his bio mom. I love Christmas shopping because all of the stores are decorated, and it's fun to pick presents out for everyone. Today, we are looking for some boots for Dad, and I think we have gone to pretty much every single Western store in town. After comparing the different ones at all of the stores, we decide on the first ones we saw, which is crazy, but at least we know these boots are the best ones.

It takes us all morning to make that one purchase, so we meet up for lunch with Carla and her mom. We are eating at our usual and favorite Mexican restaurant. Carla and I chat, excited to continue our shopping trip together. I pick the curly chips so I can scoop more queso into them, and Carla likes the ones that have the most orange seasoning on them. I always eat a million chips before my food arrives, but I still have room for more food. We don't get dessert today, though, because we want to hurry and get more shopping done.

The restaurant isn't too far from the mall, so it doesn't take us long to get there. Carla, Lily, and I are going to shop by ourselves while Mom goes with Carla's mom. We each get some money so we can buy presents. I am looking for something for Aaron. I want to get him a Christmas present, and I have no idea what to get or how much I should spend.

Carla suggests, "How about a watch?"

"Ummm, I don't know. I don't remember seeing him wear one, but maybe he doesn't want to," I say, indecisively.

"K. What about a CD of his favorite music?" Lily adds.

"We've kind of already done that, though. I was thinking about getting him a shirt. What do y'all think about that idea?" I ask them.

Carla says, "Boring," drawing out the word.

We walk around hoping to see something that strikes me as the perfect gift, but I still haven't really found anything that seems just right.

"Do y'all think it would be too much to get him one of those silver chain ID bracelets over there?" I say, pointing to a display in the window of a popular store for teens that sells clothes and some jewelry.

We all walk over to look at them more closely, and at the same time, agree saying in unison, "Awww," upon seeing they can be engraved. I have the store clerk engrave, "Mia & Aaron" on the smooth, top part, with the date on the underside. We have to pick it up in an hour. I'm so excited because I really love it. I hope he loves it too.

After shopping for a couple more hours and picking up the bracelet for Aaron, we are all exhausted when we get in the car to go home. Carla's dad dropped them off in town, so they are riding home with us.

"I love what you got for Aaron, Mia. I think he will really like it," Carla says.

"I do, too. Now we just have to find the perfect present for you to get Jamie."

We talk about what she is going to get him as we drive back home, keeping my mind occupied until I hear from Aaron.

~~~~~~~

After dropping Carla and her mom off at her house, my phone buzzes with a text from Aaron.

"Call me."

That's all it says. Why doesn't he just call me? Weird. Mom and I are still in the car on the way home though, so I have to wait a few minutes before I call so I have a chance to go in my room where I can talk privately.

"Hello?" he answers on the second ring.

"Hey. So, are you home?" I ask, thinking that if he's home it means he is safe.

He answers, "Ok. I will be home in about 30 minutes. My friends and I were just leaving the mall anyway."

"What?" I ask, confused.

"I will be careful. Bye."

He hangs up. I look at my phone, wondering what I missed. *Ok, that was really weird.* About ten minutes later, my phone rings, the screen saying "Call from Aaron."

I answer, "Are you ok? What is going on?"

"I'm fine. I just needed to pretend Mom was calling me to come home so I could leave."

"Oh; I guess that makes a little more sense. So, why couldn't you just leave anyway?"

"I didn't want to make her upset. Everything was fine, but after dinner she started talking about me moving back in with her. I felt like I needed an out."

"What? You can't move back in with her!" I say, thinking he surely knows that would be crazy.

"I'm not, Mia. I mean, I sometimes I wish I could live with my real mom and that everything would be normal and ok, but I know that's not really possible. Plus, the Alexanders are my parents now. And I have to finish school. And of course, the most important thing… there's you; I would hate not seeing you every day."

"I understand," I say, even though I really don't completely get why he would even think twice about it after what she put him through while he was growing up.

"Stop worrying about it, Mia. It was a nice visit. I'm hoping I can see her once in a while, and since the Alexanders don't know anything about it, they won't stress about it and try to stop me."

"Ok. I hope you are right, babe. It still makes me feel worried, but I want you to be happy. I'm glad it was a good visit. Did she give you a present like she said she would in the facebook message?" I ask, having wondered all day what she might give him.

"Yeah, if you can call it that. She gave me a key to her house. She's really trying to get herself together. She wants me to come back next weekend. She said she wants to give me something else, but she didn't have the money to get it yet. I told her not to worry about getting me anything. I'm just glad she seems to be doing better," Aaron says, sounding hopeful.

"Well, that's good that she is doing better. So, are you almost home yet?" I ask.

"I'm making one more stop before I go home," he tells me.

"What? Where are you going now?"

I can hear him smiling when he says, "You'll see in 3, 2, 1...," the last number sounding in stereo. I look up, and Aaron is grinning at me standing the doorway of my room. I jump up and hug him, feeling so relieved to see him and just know that he is safe. Aaron hugs me back, and then looks down at me, our faces still close, and gives me a sweet kiss.

"Babe, I'm pretty sure we just saw each other last night. You don't have to hug me as if your life depends on it, even though I do like this greeting," he says, teasingly.

"I'm just happy you are here. I didn't think we were going to see each other today. I missed you."

"I missed you, too. Maybe you could go with me next time I go see my mom. I want her to meet you."

"Ok," I say reluctantly, "if you think it would be ok."

Aaron smiles, "It will be fine, babe. Let's watch a movie or something before I have to go home."

"K," I say, smiling back, feeling happy to have such a sweet and handsome boyfriend, and trying to believe everything is really as 'fine' as he says it is.

It's the last day of school before Christmas break, and we have a half-day. The teachers all gave their finals earlier in the week, probably so they wouldn't have to grade them today. Every class is pretty much a blow-off class, which is better than doing work, but I feel like it's kind of pointless to have to be here, and would be way more fun if Aaron was in my classes with me. Finally, the last bell rings, and we are out for two weeks. *Yay!* Since all of my family lives in Coyote, I don't have to worry about travelling during Christmas. I think it would bug me to not get to open presents at my own house on Christmas morning. Plus, I'm really happy because Aaron said that since they went out of town for Thanksgiving, they aren't going to travel during Christmas.

It's kind of weird to think Christmas is less than a week away. It seems like the year has gone by quickly, and like it hasn't really been that long since it was last Christmas. This Christmas is so much more special to me, though, since Aaron and I are together. After school, he left pretty quickly saying he had things to get done. I think he and Jamie are going to Crockett to go shopping, but they are both being secretive about it.

Carla is spending the night with me, and we are going to wrap presents. She ended up buying Jamie some vintage comic books, since he collects them. Carla is bringing the wrapping paper because her mom found Christmas superhero paper, which we are both going to use. I think I might wrap Lily's present in that, too, just to be funny. I got her some pajamas and house shoes, and I got Mom a devotional book that has a message for each day. I hope they like them.

I really don't even care what I get this year. I'm so thankful to have Aaron, and of course, my family, and a home. Last Sunday at church, we put together shoe boxes to send to kids who don't get presents. In them, they had things like toothbrushes, snacks, coloring books, gloves and hats, and each one had either a boy or girl toy, like a car or a doll. It makes me happy to be able to help kids who need it, but I can't help but think about all of the kids who won't get anything, or worse, who don't have family or a safe place to live. Sometimes I wish I was rich enough to somehow give every person in the world some sort of present for Christmas. When I said that in youth, Kathy and Ken said that more than material things, we need to pray that everyone on earth will know Jesus, because He is the best gift they could ever receive. I've prayed every night this week that God will bless everyone on earth, even those who don't know him, and that He will use me to teach others about Him.

~~~~~~~~~~

On Christmas Eve, we always go to my Grandma Helen's house, to see my Dad's side of the family. She lives in a small town called Prairie about forty-five minutes from Coyote, and even though that's not that far, we don't see her as much. My dad has two brothers and a sister, but one of his brothers died when he was little. My other uncle is a lot younger than my dad; he's actually not much older than me. He enlisted into the Marine Corps right out of High School, and has been pretty much gone since. He comes back to see all of us once a year, but he met and married his wife when he was stationed at Camp LeJeune, North Carolina, and her family all lives there, so they stayed there when he was finished serving for four years. They have two kids, a little girl who is three and a boy who is one. I wish I knew them better, but at least I can see pictures on Facebook. My aunt, Tammy, lives in Prairie near Grandma. She has twin boys, age eight. I love them since they are family, but man, they drive me nuts. They are loud and always wrestling or running through Grandma's house. Last year at Christmas, Grandma got them remote control cars that they kept wrecking into each other and into our feet. I'm so glad Lily is a girl.

Grandma Helen has a friend who always makes a whole bunch of tamales for Christmas, so we have tamales, chips and dip, ham, and various desserts. I love it because the homemade tamales are delicious, and it's different than the traditional Christmas dinner we have at my other Grandma's house for lunch on Christmas day. The twins, Justin and Dustin, are playing with their stupid, new pet iguanas that they got for early Christmas presents from their dad. Their parents are divorced, so they spent the first part of Christmas break with him and his new wife. I'm seriously not loving the iguanas, and can't imagine what their dad was thinking when he got them for the boys. I mean, really? Like the boys aren't crazy and rowdy enough without having a new pet to torture everyone with? My aunt Tammy was not happy since she has to be the one to help take care of them. Tammy hates reptiles, but I guess she allowed the boys to keep them since they are so happy. Ugh.

We stay here until midnight and then head home. I'm tired, but I figure my sister and I will still get up early to open presents. Even though we are older, we love to get up early and pretend we are still little.

On the drive home from Grandma Helen's, I text Aaron, "Hey sweetie. I hope you had a good Christmas Eve. I miss you and hope we can see each other tomorrow afternoon."

He quickly replies, "It's been good so far. Haven't done much really. Going to have a Christmas lunch tomorrow with the fam and then I'll see if I can come over. Got a surprise for u."

"What is it?" I ask, excited.

"Nope – no questions. See u tomorrow. Good night babe." *I'm so gonna kick his butt. I love surprises, but I hate them at the same time. I hope he likes what I got for him.*

~~~~~~~

Lily and I get up at 6 AM like big dorks because we still get so excited about Christmas morning. We use flashlights to look under the tree to see if we can figure out what the different wrapped presents are because Mom and Dad won't let us wake them up until 7. Mom and Dad always put their presents out for each other late Christmas Eve night, too, and they put silly things on the tags. They are so weird. I see a small present wrapped perfectly in shiny, red paper on which the tag says, "To my precious Peggy Sue, from your bearded Buddy Holly," and another present that is larger that says, "To my sexy Studmuffin, from your cute Cupcake." *Alrighty then.* Lily and I look at each other and pretend to gag.

After finally opening presents, I put all of my things in my room on my bed. I got some clothes, new makeup, and some new boots that I love. They are brown cowgirl boots with turquoise and pink designs and a cross on the front. Lily got me a really cool coloring book that is for teens and a new journal. Plus, I got a ton of candy in my stocking. *Score!*

We have Christmas dinner at Grandma's and open presents. Grandma loves her scrapbook; I made it online and it has pictures of every single member of the family. I have been snapping pictures of everyone since Thanksgiving for this project. Plus, I had everyone email me their pictures, so it turned out really awesome. My cousin, Kylee, drew my name. She is five, so I figure my aunt actually picked the present out. She got me some earrings and a necklace with crosses on them. They will match my boots, so I'm super excited and really love them. Aaron texted me right after we opened presents to see what time we would be home. I told him to give me another hour, so he plans to come over at 3:00. I can't wait to see him.

~~~~~~~

I'm wearing some of my new clothes and feeling cute as I wait outside on the porch for Aaron. I can see him driving down the highway toward our house even though he's probably still a mile away. I can tell it's him though because his red truck stands out on the road in between fields. I am holding the small, wrapped gift while enjoying the relatively warm weather for December. It's 60 degrees today, so I'm happy because I can hang outside without wearing a coat. Walking down the sidewalk to meet Aaron at his truck, I see his huge smile through the windshield as he's picking up something off of the seat before he gets out. He tells me to turn around and not look at him, so I do, anxiously waiting for him to get out. All of a sudden, I feel his arms around me and see a big panda bear pillow in front of me. I squeal as I grab the panda pillow and hug it. I guess he couldn't help but notice the panda collection I have in my room. I have panda everything, including a big panda beanbag, so this pillow is perfect. I tell Aaron that I will think of him every time I sleep on it, smiling as I get on my tip toes to give him a kiss. Aaron smiles back and says, "That's not the only thing. I have one more surprise for you, but Carla and Aaron are on their way over here because it involves them, too." *What in the world could it be?*

I hand Aaron his present while we wait and tell him to open it. He grins and asks, "Superhero Christmas paper? It's too cool to open." Excitedly, I nudge him and hurry him to open it, of course making him move in slow motion just to be annoying.

When he finally sees the bracelet, he looks more serious and looks directly into my eyes before hugging me. "I love it, Mia. This is the best present I have ever gotten."

"Really? I know it's not much, but I liked that it could be engraved," feeling a little shy all of a sudden.

"I will wear it always."

"So, what else did you get for Christmas?" I ask him, trying to change the serious mood.

"I got some shoes, clothes, and a football. Oh, and I got a new phone, an IPhone, so now I will be able to actually look at the pictures and stuff you send," Aaron replies.

"Yay! I'm gonna send you a picture right now," and I take out my phone to take a selfie of the two of us together while holding my panda in front of us.

We head to the backyard to sit on the swings while waiting for Carla and Jaimie. I wonder if Carla knew they would be coming over. We are holding hands while trying to swing in sync. It's not as easy as we think it will be, and we are cracking up every time one of us jerks away from the other, while still trying to hold hands.

Aaron tells me, "Things are going so well right now, and I'm so thankful you are with me. It scares the crap out me, though."

"Why? I'm not going anywhere, babe," I reassure him.

"It's just...Christmas was never a very fun holiday for us growing up. At school, the teachers and kids were always excited as they looked forward to the break and to getting presents. My brother and I were usually home alone for the most part, and we didn't even always have food. I would try to tell my brother that Santa sometimes got so busy that not all kids got presents every year because I was scared he would be disappointed if Mom forgot to get him anything. I didn't care about me, just him. I always tried to find something I could give him on Christmas day, and would make him whatever I could find for a meal. The crappy thing was, it was usually better if Mom wasn't there because if she was there, she was usually drunk and either she made us stay quiet, or she would cry and act like she was so sorry that she screwed up yet again. It sucked," Aaron confesses, his head down.

"I'm so sorry, babe. I can't even imagine that. Everything is going to be better from now on. I promise."

"The thing is, Mia, you can't promise that. You just never know what can happen, but I am definitely going to try to make sure that we always stay together because having you makes everything better."

Aaron reaches across the gap in between our swings, since now we are still, saying, "Come here." I lean toward him, and we kiss each other. *I really love him. Please God, make everything better for Aaron from now on.*

Our foreheads are touching, as we are looking at each other and enjoying the romantic moment right when Carla and Jaimie come around the back of the house and yell, "Get a room!"

"Whatever!" I reply, feeling my face blush. They are such buttheads. I'm happy that they are here, though, because now I can finally know what the big secret surprise is. Aaron seems to change his mood quickly, or at least hide how he was feeling before. He smiles and gets up to give Jamie a fist bump. I look at Carla, "Do you know what's going on?" to which she shakes her head, "nope!"

The guys smile and tell us we are going to take a walk so we can sit on our tractor tire, which is quickly becoming our usual spot to hang out. Once there, the guys smile and pull out envelopes from their back pockets. They hand them to Carla and me, and tell us to open them together at the count of three. "One, two, THREE," the boys say in unison, and Carla and I quickly open the envelopes, both screaming when we see tickets to Aerosmith!

"Oh my gosh Aaron! How did you get these? I haven't heard about any concerts coming!"

"That's because it's in Dallas during Spring Break. Jamie and I asked y'all's parents if they would let us all go to Dallas together during Spring Break, and they all agreed, so we bought the tickets online," Aaron explains, grinning hugely. Carla and I both give Jaimie and Aaron huge hugs as we continue to squeal in excitement. *I cannot believe this! I am SO excited! Woohoo!*

Chapter 10
January

January is actually when it really starts getting colder around here. It's neat that it's a new year and everything, but it is always so gray outside and everything around seems dead and quiet. Plus, it means starting back to school after two weeks off, which is always hard.

Aaron, Carla, and Jamie got to come to our house for New Year's Eve, along with Lily's friend. My parents went on a date, so we had the house to ourselves. Mom bought us some confetti popper things to use at midnight, and we played dance games on the Wii and sang karaoke while waiting for the New Year. At around 11:45, we watched the ball drop on TV, although we weren't watching it live because of the time change. It had actually happened in New York an hour before us. We all stood around in the living room counting down from 10, and as soon as we yelled "1," Aaron kissed me while Lily and her friend were screaming and popping confetti and streamer things into the air. I could feel him smile while our lips still touched, and he whispered, "Happy New Year, Mia." I said it back, and then popped a confetti popper right at him. We were both laughing, and everyone was running around the living room yelling and picking up the confetti off of the floor to throw at each other again. It was so fun.

As soon as we started back to school, though, the cold mood of the first of the year took over. My classes seem to take so much longer, and the teachers are worried about making sure we are prepared for the STAAR tests that are, "just around the corner." Aaron is on the basketball team, and they play twice a week. I am able to go to the home games, but it seems like there are more away games than anything. Aaron has to practice with the team after school every day, so we only get to really see each other on the weekends.

By the third weekend of the month, the team finally has a Friday off, so Aaron is taking me to a movie. It feels like we haven't seen each other in forever with everything going on. I'm wearing one of my new outfits that I got for Christmas with my new boots, along with some of my new makeup. I feel pretty good about myself as I look into the mirror in my bathroom. I have to stand on the side of the bathtub to get a full view of myself in the bathroom mirror, so of course, I have the door shut so nobody sees me.

Mom and Dad are in the living room so I wait for Aaron in there with them, occasionally peeking out the window to see if he's coming yet. Mom says, "You look cute in your new clothes, Mia!"

"Thanks, Momma!"

Then Dad has to tease me because he can't help himself, "Let me mess up your hair a little; you can't be too pretty on a date, or I'll have to have a talk with Aaron before y'all leave."

"Dad...." I say, trying to make him stop, but I know he's just teasing, so I smile and keep watching for Aaron.

Finally, Aaron pulls up, and comes to get me at the door. He's wearing the bracelet I got him and a nice button-up shirt with jeans. He looks super cute. He told me the other day that he's only taken the bracelet off for basketball games because they aren't allowed to wear anything like that for safety reasons. Dad continues with his orneriness by announcing Aaron's arrival as soon as Aaron walks in the door, yelling, "Nerd alert! Nerd alert!" Thankfully, Aaron knows my dad is a big dork, so it doesn't bother him.

In Aaron's truck, I scoot close to him and sit in the middle seat, my favorite place to be, especially since it's freezing outside. I can cuddle with Aaron all the way to Crockett. Aaron picks the movie this time, and we see the new action/suspense movie where a girl gets kidnapped and her boyfriend saves her. I jump and hide my face in Aaron's chest half the movie, freaking out every time there is a scary scene. Aaron just laughs at me, so I throw a piece of popcorn at his face. He opens his mouth and tries to catch the next piece, and we giggle quietly so we hopefully won't get kicked out.

After the movie, we go to a neat little hamburger restaurant that is decorated in kind of a rugged way, with wood and tin accents. Everyone writes on the walls so it's cool to read what people write. They actually have silver sharpies on the tables so people can add whatever they want, so Aaron picks up our Sharpie, takes the lid off, and writes on the wall beside our booth, "Aaron loves Mia!" He draws a big heart around it and then hands me the marker saying, "You're turn," smiling. I'm just looking at him, wide-eyed, so he asks, "What?"

He hasn't told me he loves me out loud. Is this the same? Does he really love me? I mean, I know he likes me...and I know I do love him. Should I ask him about it?

"Mia..." Aaron snaps in my face, trying to get my attention. "Hellooo? You OK?"

I realize I'm spacing, so I try to smile, and take the marker from him without saying anything. He watches me as I write on the wall beside me, "Mia loves Aaron too!" with a big heart around it just like his. I look at him, and he leans across the booth and grabs each side of my face to pull me in for a kiss. Neither one of us says anything more about it during dinner nor on the ride home, but inside, I'm feeling elated.

The next day, Saturday, Aaron has to help his dad around the house, so he tells me he will see me tomorrow at church. I love that his family goes to our church now. They seem like they have always gone there; I think they know everyone already, maybe more people than I even know there.

At church, Aaron seems a little distant but says he's just tired. He tells me he can't go to youth tonight because he has homework. I'm disappointed, but at least we got to see each other and have fun on Friday. Youth was really good tonight, though, so I hate that he missed it. Ken talked about how like the winter weather, we have to die to ourselves and let go of our sins so that Christ can create us in a new way. He cites:

> There is a time for everything,
> and a season for every activity under the heavens:
> a time to be born and a time to die,
> a time to plant and a time to uproot,
> a time to kill and a time to heal,
> a time to tear down and a time to build,
> a time to weep and a time to laugh,
> a time to mourn and a time to dance,
> a time to scatter stones and a time to gather them,
> a time to embrace and a time to refrain from embracing,
> a time to search and a time to give up,
> a time to keep and a time to throw away,
> a time to tear and a time to mend,
> a time to be silent and a time to speak,
> a time to love and a time to hate,
> a time for war and a time for peace.
> Ecclesiastes 3: 1-8

We broke into small groups and thought of different examples of things we need to let go of and how God can keep molding us into who He wants us to be. Ken said that even though winter seems bleak and dreary, that really, it is a season of rest and is important for getting rid of the old so the new and improved can emerge. God can use every season in our lives on which to build, even the times that seem discouraging and awful.

I know I am supposed to apply what we learn to myself, but I can't help but think of Aaron and his past and how he worries about it affecting who he is today in a negative way. I can't really imagine how I would feel in his place, though. It's very hard for me to understand how he can still want to see his mom, even if he does forgive her for everything she did. She doesn't treat him nicely, or at least the times I was around, it didn't seem like she was very nice.

At home in bed Sunday night, I pray that God will help Aaron see himself the way God sees him, and that God will guide Aaron throughout the seasons in his life.

~~~~~~~

The following week the boys' basketball team is playing at home on Friday, so Carla and I go and sit in the stands to watch. Our fans are all stomping in the stands and screaming as the opposing team is shooting a free throw the last minute of the game. We are winning, 72-70, so the close game has created a lot of excitement in both sides of the stands. Aaron is not a starter in basketball, but he is in because three of our players have fouled out. It is intense when the ball leaves the player's hands, only to bounce off of the backboard and straight into the net. The score becomes 72-71, and there are 50 seconds left on the clock. He misses the second free throw, so our crowd is cheering while at the same time holding our breaths as we watch our team head to their end of the court. The ball is passed around back and forth from post to point as our team tries to wait out the clock, but all of a sudden, one of the other team's players steals the ball, and makes it to his basket for a clean lay-up. The crowd is silent on our side since we only have 5 seconds left, and the opposing team just pulled ahead. When Aaron throws the ball in, our team is spread out down the court hoping to pass it as closely as they can to have a chance to make the basket. He throws it to the middle of the court to a player who, instead of trying to pass it, turns to the basket and shoots for a half court basket. Sadly, he misses, and the buzzer indicates the game over and a win for the other team, who all run out to the middle of the court in excitement.

After the game, Aaron smiles at me as he leaves the dressing room. He is disappointed in the loss but not too worried about it.

"So, what do you want to do?" I ask him. "I'm so glad it's finally Friday night."

"Well, I actually told my bio mom I would come to town and see her. Mom and Dad think I'm hanging out with friends after the game. You wanna come?"

"Oh, wow...ummm, I guess I can go with you. Do you think we will be back in time for my curfew?" I ask, nervously.

"We will definitely be back because I told Mom and Dad I would be home by midnight. We can just go and see her for an hour and then come back," he reassures me.

"Ok, cool. Let me tell Carla real quick, and I will meet you at your truck."

Carla is still talking to Jamie over by the concession stand. He had to work in there tonight to help raise money for the senior class, and it takes a while to clean everything up after games. Carla pouts when I tell her we are going to town without them, but I tell her that Aaron wants to take me to get ice cream by ourselves. I can't tell her the truth, and I hate it.

When we get to Crockett, Aaron turns into a neighborhood west of town, where the houses look pretty run down. It's dark with no street lights, but there are people out sitting on front porches or around their cars, and I feel nervous and out of place. Aaron puts his hand on my knee, sensing my anxiety, and we end up stopping at the end of the street at a small, white house with chipped paint and a sagging roof.

"Is this it? Is there where she lives?" I ask, trying not to sound the way I feel, because I really don't want to offend Aaron.

"Yeah, it looks bad but it's a little better on the inside," he answers.

We go up to the door and knock. I stand behind Aaron on the narrow sidewalk leading up to the door. His mom opens it and motions for us to come in, without saying anything. Aaron breaks the silence though, and greets his mom, "Hey, Mom, this is Mia, my girlfriend."

I smile timidly but reach out my hand to shake hers, and she gives me her hand, limply shaking mine back. "Hey," she addresses me, and then tells us to have a seat. I look around at the dim living room, and we sit on an old, yellow couch that looks like it's from the 70's. She sits on the only other chair in the room, a brown leather chair on which duct tape mends multiple rips. There is a 13 inch box TV on a TV tray, but it's not on.

This is going to be a really long hour.

Aaron starts a conversation by telling his mom about the basketball game. She seems distracted but nods here and there. She tells him she got a job but that she lost it after a week because the boss was a jerk, and doesn't elaborate further. It's silent again for a few minutes, and then his mom jumps up quickly, offering us some water. It's like she all of a sudden realized she should be a host. Without waiting for a reply, she makes her way a couple of steps into the kitchen and fills two glasses with tap water. We thank her, and she sits back down, kind of looking around and not really looking at us. I decide to try to talk, hating the awkwardness, and compliment her picture on the wall. It stands out on the paneling considering it is a snow scene with mountains in the background. She kind of nods at me and looks at the picture as she mumbles a thank you.

His mom is wearing tight, faded jeans with a skimpy black tank top. She's really skinny, and her bleach-blonde hair with dark roots hangs about half-way down her back. It seems like she might be freezing since it's so cold outside, but I notice a small, electric heater in the corner, and it seems to be doing a pretty good job of heating the small living room.

After another thirty minutes of intermittent small talk, Aaron stands up and reaches his hand down to me to help me up, telling his mom that we need to get back. Aaron's mom asks if she can talk to him privately for a minute, so he gives me the keys to the truck and tells me he will be there in a second. I hesitantly head to the truck and get in, starting it so it will hopefully heat up quickly, and locking the doors until he comes out. Thankfully, he opens the door to her house, and I see him tell her bye before heading to the truck. I quickly unlock the door so he can climb in the truck, wondering what she needed to tell him that I couldn't hear.

"Is everything Ok?" I ask, hoping he will tell me what's going on.

"Yes; she just needed to borrow a little money since she lost her job," he tells me, while backing out of her driveway. I look at the clock on my phone and it is 11:30, so I feel glad that we will make it home in time.

"Did you give her some?"

"Yeah, I had $20 and gave her that, but I told her I might be able to help more later because she said she really needed $50 instead," he says.

"Are you able to do that?" I ask, since he doesn't work.

He nods his head yes and tells me has some saved up from allowance. He says she told him she would pay him back, but I silently doubt that. We head home while listening to the radio, and Aaron drives up to the school where I left my car parked. He gives me a kiss and hug and smiles, telling me, "Thank you for coming, babe. I'm really glad you were able to meet my mom. I know it was kind of awkward, but I'm just glad to see her doing better. She hadn't been drinking or anything, so I'm really happy about that."

"Thank you for inviting me. It means a lot to me that you trust me enough to let me come with. I will pray for her that she can keep doing better," I say.

"Thank you," Aaron says as he opens the driver's side door of my car to let me in. It's five minutes until midnight, so I hurry and start the car so I can go. Aaron leans down to give me one more kiss before we both head home.

Chapter 11
February

The halls and lockers in the high school are all decorated with pink and red hearts announcing a fundraiser that the Student Council is doing. They are doing the usual "Choco-heart" sales where everyone can purchase a chocolate heart to be delivered to his or her significant other or friend, but this year, they are also doing something new, and it's hilarious. Beside the school office, there is a long table with multiple jars with pictures on them of the principal and some of the teachers and coaches. The person's jar that has the most money in it by the end of the week will be the one who is going to be hypnotized by a comedian at an assembly on Friday, which is Valentine's Day.

On Friday morning, it looks close between Principal Phillips and Coach Martin. *Oh My Gosh! It would be awesome to see Coach Martin be made to do stupid things.* I put all of my change In hls jar and head to class. During third period, there is a knock on the door, and Josh comes in dressed as Cupid to deliver Choco-hearts. He looks so funny with facial hair and wings. He hands the first one to me, so I read the little card attached to it:

"To my Sweet Valentine, Mia. Love, Aaron."

I smile and feel happy that he got me one. I had one sent to him, too, so I hope he enjoys getting it, but I also got him something else for Valentine's Day. I will give it to him after school, though.

Thankfully, basketball season is over, so we already made plans to hang out.

The assembly is last period, and everyone meets in the auditorium. We don't have to sit with our classes, so Carla, Jamie, Aaron, and I all sit together. We got pretty good seats, front row right in the middle, because the guys got there early. Everyone is talking and being silly, when Mr. Phillips begins to shush everyone from behind the microphone, "Quiet down everyone. Settle down." It gets quiet enough for him to continue:

"Alright, as everyone knows, we had a big contest all week to see who gets to be hypnotized in front of everyone by the great, Harry the Hypnotizer. Can I get a drum roll please?" he asks, and the whole student body pats their legs. He waits while the secretary walks to him to give him the results, and he opens it and smiles, while yelling in a game show host voice, "Coach Martin!"

Yes! This is gonna be good.

The curtains open and on the stage is a man who looks pretty normal, in jeans and a t-shirt. He smiles as he invites Coach Martin to the stage to sit on the single chair in the middle of the stage. The spotlight is on him, and the rest of the lights in the auditorium are dimmed as Harry the Hypnotizer begins his show. I kind of expected the guy to be weird looking or somehow dressed up, but his being dressed like any other person actually makes him seem more credible.

"Coach Martin, I want you to listen to the sound of my voice and focus on your breathing," Harry says, achieving an eye-roll from Coach Martin and a laugh from the audience.

"Think about a place where you are most happy and comfortable and close your eyes." Harry tells Coach Martin to relax and talks to him with a soothing voice until it appears that Coach is resting his head on his chest like he fell asleep in the chair. Harry touches Coach on the shoulder and tells him to picture himself flying like Superman. He tells Coach that it is a peaceful and fun flight and tells him he needs to get up and fly around the room. Coach sits there for a minute, and I can hear my friends speculating whether or not this is real.

All of a sudden, Coach gets up and with his hands out like he's flying, he starts circling the stage. Harry says, "Watch out for the mountains! You crashed in the nearby ocean, so you need to swim to the island." Coach Martin falls to the ground and starts making swimming motions. Harry continues, "Ok, you have reached the island. You can explore." Coach is looking around and acting like he's very interested in whatever he is seeing. "You've come upon a family of monkeys and the only way they won't hurt you is if you act like one of them." The audience giggles as Coach Martin starts making crazy sounds while walking hunched over like a monkey. I can't decide if this is real or not. Coach isn't laughing, so if he is pretending, he sure is doing a good job.

After making Coach climb island trees among other tasks, Harry instructs him to swim to a boat that has come to rescue him. Coach pretends to swim and looks genuinely happy to be saved. Harry has Coach sit back on the chair and brings him back to his happy place.

"Ok, Coach. You are feeling so relaxed and happy, and I want you to think about all of your students. Every single student you have has earned a free one hundred because they have all agreed to never discuss your trip to the island with you," Harry says while looking into the crowd smiling and putting his finger over his mouth telling us to keep it quiet.

The crowd cheers and after Harry counts backwards from 10 to 1, Coach Martin wakes up slowly. He rolls his eyes again while the crowd quietly waits to see how he reacts to everything that just happened.

"How do you feel Coach Martin?" Harry asks, smiling.

"I feel like you won't be able to hypnotize me," Coach responds with a smirk.

"You're probably right," Harry says, but then he addresses the students, "Well guys, Coach doesn't think he can be hypnotized. I guess since it's time for school to be out now, I will let Coach dismiss you."

Coach Martin looks at his watch and looks confused since he obviously doesn't remember the last forty minutes. Everyone is cracking up as Coach stands up and tells us to have a good weekend. He acts like nothing happened and walks off the stage.

Aaron grabs my hand as we leave the auditorium making our way through the crowd of students who are all riled up and acting crazy. Once we get to the parking lot, I ask him if he thinks Coach was really hypnotized. Aaron laughs and shrugs his shoulders, "Who knows? It was weird but at least it was funny, much better than class." I agree and hug him, excited about our evening.

Aaron winks at me and with our foreheads touching, he whispers, "Can't wait for tonight. I feel like I've missed you. I'll pick you up at 6:30. I have a few things to do first."

"Ok, babe! I'll be ready and waiting," I say, smiling as I jump in my jeep to head home.

~~~~~~~

I had planned to wear a cute, new skirt and shirt that Mom got me the other day, but Aaron texted me and said not to dress up.

Weird. I assumed a Valentine's date would be something where we would dress up a little more.

Looking through my closet, I'm struggling to find cute but non-dressy clothes that are clean. My dirty clothes pile is kind of huge because I haven't taken it to the laundry room. I finally decide to wear a pair of older jeans that have a hole in the knee, and I throw on a black and pink t-shirt that is form fitting. It's cold outside, though, so I decide to wear a jean jacket that is the same color as the jeans. Even though it is super casual, I think I look pretty cute. Aaron is supposed to be at my house in 10 minutes, so I freshen up my makeup and head to the living room to wait for him.

Carla texted and said she and Jamie are going out to eat and to a movie. I told her I'm not sure what we are doing yet, but I'm sure it will be fun since I will be with Aaron.

At 6:45, Aaron is still not here, so I decide to text him to make sure everything is ok.

"Hey, r u on ur way yet?"

At 7:00, I still haven't gotten a reply, and I'm starting to get upset. It's not really like Aaron to just ignore me or take forever to respond. Mom and Dad went on a date, and Lily is spending the night with all of her friends who don't have dates. They are having some kind of Valentine's slumber party; Lily has been saying it would be more fun to hang out with her friends than to go on a "stupid" date. I think she's just jealous, but she probably will have fun. I bet she's having more fun than me right now, since I'm sitting here in my living room alone and feeling a little freaked out that I haven't heard from Aaron and he's late.

At 7:15 I finally get a text:

"Sorry – running late. On way now."

I'm having a hard time not feeling gripey and mad at him, even though I'm still excited to see him.

He's acting weird, and it makes me nervous.

At 7:30, I finally hear Aaron's truck pulling up, but instead of meeting him outside, I decide to wait for him to come to the door. He rings the doorbell, and I take a few minutes to open the door, my way of punishing him a little for being late. He's standing on the porch with his hands in his pockets of his jeans, looking at the ground, until he sees the door open. He looks up at me with a timid smile, and before I can even get out the door, he's pulling me to him into a huge hug, telling me he's sorry. It's hard to stay gripey when my super-hot boyfriend is hugging me and apologizing, so I smile into his neck and hug him back, telling him it's ok. He smells so good to me-- like love, if love has a scent. Hopefully he doesn't notice me smelling him, though. I don't want him to think I'm creepy or anything.

Hand in hand, we walk to his truck and Aaron starts driving without saying where we are going. I asked him, but he just smiled and said it's a surprise.

I sure hope it involves food because I am STAR-stinkin-VING!

Aaron looks at me and squeezes my hand, then back at the road, asking, "What are you thinking, Mia?"

"Oh nothing. Just wondering where we are going, since SOMEBODY won't tell me." I smile back and lay my head on his shoulder. I love riding in his truck with him since we can sit so close together.

Aaron chuckles and shakes his head, "Nope, not gonna work. You will see soon enough."

I reach down and turn the radio up, singing along with the song, *All About That Bass*, by Meghan Trainor. Aaron looks at me with his eyebrows up, "Really???"

I laugh and say, "Yep this is my new song. I'm bringin' booty back."

He shakes his head and laughs while I keep singing and dancing in my seat. Aaron continues to drive but clearly thinks I'm crazy. This is not the usual kind of music we listen to, but it's a fun song. After it's over, he tells me, "Well, at least it gives me a chance to see your mad dancing skills, and you *are* perfect, just like the song says."

I laugh, but I definitely enjoy the compliment. When we get to Crockett, Aaron seems to be headed towards the older part of the city, where there are actually brick roads. I know there is an area of this part of town that has bars and places where college people hang out, but I can't think of where we might be going. All of a sudden, we pull up to a huge metal building that has been here forever, and I realize we are at the old skating rink. I thought it was only open for parties, though, but there are cars here. I look at Aaron, and he smiles and takes my hand as I jump out of his side of the truck.

"Dude! Are we going skating?"

"Yep," Aaron says, without really giving me much more information.

"I thought this place was closed down. I'm so excited! I haven't been skating since I was in elementary school," I happily reply.

When we enter, the place looks different from what I remember. It is kind of dark, but as we get further in, there is one end of the building that has tables with white table cloths and candles on them. There are maybe 30 couples here, all at their own tables, and the waiters are actually wearing skates as they deliver food and drinks. There is a banner on the way to the tables that says Valentine's Couples Night. *Oh my gosh. This is too cool!*

Aaron has apparently reserved our table, and the hostess shows us to our seats. There are already skates sitting next to our chairs, and glow jewelry as a centerpiece on the table beside the candle. We each get a glow necklace and bracelet and put them on.

"How did you know about this?" I ask Aaron, since I have never heard of them doing something like it.

"I've got my sources," Aaron smirks, as the waiter brings us our drinks. Apparently the food was pre-ordered because everyone is getting a plate with chicken fried steak, green beans, mashed potatoes, and a big dinner roll. I figure it is catered. Aaron knew to order me a diet Dr.Pepper, so I take a drink while we wait for our food. There is music playing already, but I guess everyone will skate after eating. It's interesting because the different couples in here are all different ages. There is one couple sitting to our right who appears to be in their sixties. They are dressed up like hippies, with bell bottoms and flowery shirts. I guess they wanted to make tonight seem like when they were younger.

"This is so cool! I love it!"

"I'm glad you like it. I thought it sounded fun and it was something different to do, since it's cold outside, and there isn't a ton of stuff to do around here," Aaron says.

"I wondered what on earth you were planning when you told me to not dress up. So, why were you late to pick me up?" I ask Aaron, hoping he will tell me.

"I just had a few things I had to do around the house first. No big deal."

"Well, I'm so excited we are getting to do this. I seriously hope I don't fall, though. I wasn't the best skater in the world when I was young, and since I haven't done this in forever, I'm a little nervous."

"I'll be right there with you. For a while when I was like 6 or 7, we lived near here, and sometimes the owner would let me help him out so that I could get in for free. I fixed skates, tightened wheels, helped people find sizes, that sort of thing. Anything was better than being at home, and mom didn't know or care what I was doing or where I was. This was before my brother was born, so I didn't have to stay home and help take care of him," Aaron shares, revealing a little more about his childhood.

"How old were you when CPS took y'all?"

"It was the end of 4th grade, so I had just turned 10. The lady came to the school and said she was going to take me to live with a really nice family because my mother needed help. I loved to draw so I put all of my drawings in my best friend's locker. I didn't get to say goodbye. It pretty much sucked."

"Wow, that's terrible," I say, not sure how to respond.

Just then, our food arrives, so Aaron smiles and says, "That's enough talking about that. This night is special, and I want to focus on you." Aaron picks up his drink and we toast with our big, red, plastic Coca-Cola cups. "To us," Aaron says, and I reply, "To us," smiling.

Since other people had gotten their food before us, several couples have made their way to the skating area. There is a huge disco ball in the middle and other lights shining all over the floor. There are a few people who are going really slowly and cracking up as they re-learn to skate, but that older Hippy couple is skating hand-in-hand together speeding past everyone. It's kind of funny. I hope Aaron and I will be like that when we are older because they are clearly having fun.

After eating, we lace up our skates. The skates are actually the old kind, brown with four orange wheels and an orange bumper thing in the front to use as a brake. They are super heavy, and I'm not sure my ankles are strong enough to support them, but maybe once I get going, it will get easier. Aaron leads me around the edge to the opening where we can enter the skating rink. I'm moving very slowly, and Aaron is coaxing me along. "Come on,

Mia. You've got this. Just hold my hands and I will lead you," Aaron says, skating backwards while pulling me along. I'm smiling nervously, but this is actually really fun. As I kind of remember how to move faster, Aaron turns and skates beside me instead. So far the music has been different types, and this one is an old song, probably for the old couple. It's a fast song so we go pretty fast, the wind blowing my hair back. It's such a freeing feeling to be gliding along, almost like flying while still attached to the ground, if that makes sense.

They actually have a few little competitions throughout the evening. I don't mind standing on the side while Aaron joins. I laugh watching Aaron play the limbo. He skates under a string that seems like it's maybe two feet off of the ground. One of his legs is out and one is bent and he is laying back really far. It's totally crazy that he can do it, but I cheer for him when he wins, and he brings me a stuffed teddy bear that's holding a heart, his prize for winning. We go to the table to chill for a bit and to rest since skating is way more of a workout than I remember. Plus, we need a drink.

"Oh my gosh, babe! I'm having the best time!" I tell Aaron after I carefully sit/slide into my seat with my skates still on. I don't know how in the world the waiters can carry drinks and food while on skates. I would seriously bust it. They sure get around fast, though, and have already refilled our drinks, thank goodness.

Aaron kind of smiles back at me, and reaches into his pocket, pulling out a small, white box with a red ribbon around it. He says, "Mia, you mean the world to me. You know that, right?" I nod and smile nervously back as our conversation is getting more serious. "I'm so thankful we are together. You have been there for me and have helped me to realize that even though I come from a crazy past, I can still move forward, and I want to do that with you. I love you, babe." *Oh my gosh!!! He totally just said it out loud for the first time.*

"Oh my gosh, babe! I love you, too! I've been scared to say it because I didn't want you to think I was clingy or weird or too serious," I ramble.

Aaron hands me the box, and I look at it and then up at him again. "My present for you is at home. I'm sorry. I didn't realize I should have brought it with me."

"It's ok. Open it," Aaron urges me.

I untie the bow and pull the lid off of the box. Removing a piece of cotton, I see a beautiful bracelet with a heart and a cross dangling from it. The silver chain holds a smooth, silver, small cross, and next to it dangles a red, ruby heart.

"This is so pretty, Aaron! Thank you so much!"

"You're welcome. When I saw it, I immediately thought of you. Let me help you put it on," Aaron says as he clasps it around my wrist.

I touch it, holding the charms so that I can see them better. It really is so pretty.

The skating rink is only going to be open for thirty more minutes, so we skate/dance to a couple more slow songs before leaving. When I take my skates off, if feels like I'm still moving and skating. It's really weird. Aaron laughs at me as I get my footing; "You are so funny, Mia. I didn't think I would have to hold on to you while you are wearing normal shoes, too!"

I smack his arm, "Ha ha ha! You are SO hilarious!"

I love him holding on to me any time, though, so I can take a little teasing. Maybe I should wobble all of the time like I'm going to fall so he can have plenty of chances to be there to catch me. He might start wondering what the heck is wrong with me, though, so I just kind of smile while lost in my silly thought.

Back in the truck, Aaron cranks up the heater and plays the radio softly as we drive back to my house. We are actually pretty quiet for the most part, I guess both of us thinking. I wonder what Aaron is thinking about, though. I hope he's not sad thinking about our discussion earlier. It's like, I want to know more about him, but I want to be careful not to upset him.

When we get to my house, I tell Aaron to wait outside for a second so I can run in and get his present. I carry it behind my back, and caution him as I walk down the sidewalk to where he is leaning against the front of his truck, his headlights still on so we can see.

"Babe, I didn't get anything as nice as what you got me. I'm sorry. I hope you like it, though."

Aaron shakes his head and smiles, "You are my best present! I don't need anything else."

Ummm, how does he always make my heart flutter like that?

"Ok. Close your eyes!" I hand him a huge stuffed ape that actually sings and dances. It is holding a heart that says, "Ape for you."

I press the ape's hand and it starts singing, "I'm Yours," by Jason Mraz. At least I was able to download my own song onto it, so it didn't sing something weird. I put the ape in Aaron's hand and instruct him to open his eyes. Laughing, he starts dancing with it and singing along. I can feel myself blush because I know it is lame compared to what he gave me, but Aaron puts it on the hood of his truck so it can finish singing, while grabbing me into his arms for a huge hug. "Mia, I freaking love you! The ape is great, but you are awesome!" I can feel him talk into my hair while he continues to hug me tight.

"I love you, too, Aaron, forever!"   We stand in front of his headlights with the ape singing again and dance slowly, while still lost in our tight embrace.

Chapter 12
March

I am SO freakin' excited that in only two weeks, we will be in Dallas for the Aerosmith concert! This is going to be the best spring break I've ever had. Carla and I have been planning what we will wear, and we decided we want to both wear our black, skinny jeans with similar high-heeled, black sandals that we bought together last weekend. We are going to paint our toenails red and rat up our hair to make it really big. We ordered Aerosmith t-shirts online for all four of us, and the girl shirts we got are both fitted and black and red, but they have different pictures on them. We actually got the boys shirts that sort of match ours. I am going to wear red lipstick and red, hoop earrings, and I plan to wear my black eyeliner kind of dark and going outward a little from my eyes. Carla and I are going for a modern version of the 80's rocker girl look, and I think we will look super cute! We are both just a little obsessed with the whole thing, so getting through the next two weeks of school is going to suck.

~~~~~~~

Sitting in band today, I am kind of daydreaming about Aaron and our upcoming trip when Mr. Cunningham has apparently been trying to get my attention for several minutes. *Embarrassing!*

"I'm sorry, sir. Could you repeat that?" I ask, with my face stupidly turning bright red. Ugh. I hate that my face reveals my feelings. I hear a couple of people in the class giggle, and Mr. Cunningham looks at me like he's a little annoyed at having to repeat himself, but he does anyway.

"I said, since you are band president, Mia, I need you to help with the spring fundraiser. Can you please come up here and explain what we are doing to raise money for new uniforms?"

"Oh, umm, of course...sorry."

I get up and walk a couple of feet to where Mr. Cunningham stands to direct the band. Since I play flute, we sit in an arc that makes the first row of the band, closest to him, as the rest of the band sits in arcs behind us.

I don't love talking in front of everyone. You would think that since I'm involved in a million different extracurricular things that I would be really outgoing, but I'm actually pretty much an introvert. I've heard that public speaking is considered a bigger fear than death for many people. I'm thinking I might not go to that extreme, considering I'm up here about to talk, but I figuratively feel like I could die when my voice comes out higher pitched, and I talk really fast because of my stupid nerves. Plus, my face is still red, so I can just imagine how cute that must look. *This is just lovely. Why do I always want to be president of everything?*

"Ok, everyone. So, everyone knows our uniforms are really crappy..." Before I can continue, Mr. Cunningham interrupts by clearing his throat. I look at him, and rephrase what I'm saying; "Oh...umm, I mean, we all know our uniforms are not in great condition anymore." Mr. Cunningham nods his head in approval, so I keep going. I notice Aaron smiling in the back, and try to conceal my smile. I guess I didn't think "crappy" was that bad of a word.

"So, this is what we are going to do, or at least, it's the first of probably quite a few fundraisers that we need to do so that we can get new uniforms. I know everyone is sick of selling things all the time, so we thought maybe this would work better, and be more fun at the same time. Since we don't have a movie theater in our town and the nearest one is thirty minutes away, we thought we could have movie nights in the gym. We have a big projector so we are able to make it like the real movies, and we are going to have a concession stand like they do at the theater. We will sell tickets at The Store as well as at school and also to our families and friends. The school board has given us permission to use the gym on several Friday nights throughout the rest of the school year, and then we were thinking we could have outdoor movie nights during the summer and project the movie on the wall outside of the band hall. It would be a perfect spot because people could bring their own chairs or blankets and put them in the parking lot to watch the movie. What do y'all think?"

Everyone seems excited, and starts shouting out different movies we could show for the first one. I explain that each movie will be family friendly so that everyone will want to come.

I give everyone the details, like ticket prices and stuff, and then the bell rings indicating the end of the school day.

I'm glad everyone seems to be excited and likes the idea. I think it will be fun, and will be a neat change for our little town. Since everyone kind of knows everyone in this town, it will be a really fun social gathering for young people and also for older members of the community.

~~~~~~~

We've been selling tickets for the Friday movie for almost two weeks and we are expecting around 200 people to show up tonight. Today is the start of spring break, so the whole school has been super excited about our upcoming week off, and for tonight's movie. It's a good thing we aren't leaving for our Dallas trip until Wednesday.

Just in ticket sales, the band has made over $500, and with the concession stand and people paying at the door tonight, we are hoping to double that. It's a great start to getting better uniforms. At least for my senior year, maybe I will have a uniform that fits right, and even though I realize band uniforms aren't exactly made to make people look hot, I hope I won't look ridiculous like I have in the past.

I have to be at the gym early to help prepare for the crowd, and there are about twenty other band members here helping as well. Aaron was supposed to be here by now, so I keep watching the door for him. The movie will start in thirty minutes and there are a bunch of people here already, many who are in line for snacks at the concession stand. I'm kind of glad I am not working the concession stand tonight. Thankfully, band parents have stepped in to help with that and also with selling tickets at the door. My job is to just kind of act like a host and welcome people. Several of the older people in the community are here tonight just to be supportive. We decided to set tables up outside of the gym so people could have coffee and talk, so I figure many of the older people will just sit at the tables and chat instead of watch the movie. Many people have told me how great an idea this is, and I feel very excited and proud that our band is not only raising money, but at the same time, doing something really fun for our community.

I'm still very distracted by the fact that Aaron hasn't made it yet, though. Carla and Jamie have already gone into the gym to find seats, and they are supposed to be saving seats for us so we can all sit together. I can see through the gym windows that the lights have been turned off and the movie is fixing to start, so I go ahead and go find Carla. She texted me and said they are sitting on the 4th row on the right, so I don't have too much trouble finding them. I texted Aaron several times asking him if he's on his way, but I haven't heard anything back yet. I don't know whether to be mad or worried, and I'm reminded of his being late for our Valentine's date. *Ugh. Where are you, babe?*

After the movie has been on for like 30 minutes, Aaron finally slips in to the seat next to me. He grabs my hand, and whispers, "Hey, sorry I'm late."

"What happened? Where were you?" I whisper back.

"I'll tell you later," he says, looking up at the screen, effectively postponing our discussion. I'm having a really hard time not feeling irritated, but man, I'm so glad he's here. I rest my head on his shoulder, and we continue to hold hands throughout the rest of the movie.

When the movie ends, it's kind of funny because everyone claps. I guess we are kind of country around here. The lights come on, and I squint as my eyes adjust from the darkness to the bright lights in the gym. It's crowded as people leave, so we all slowly make our way out to our cars. Aaron walks with me to my car and jumps in with me so we can chat for a little while before he has to go home.

He starts to kiss me, and even though I love it and I kiss him back, I quickly pull away, feeling like I don't exactly want people to see us since there are still many people around talking and taking while to leave.

"Dude! People will see us," I laugh, explaining my embarrassment as reason for pulling away.

Aaron chuckles, replying, "Don't freak out, babe. I don't care who sees us. You are mine, so they can deal with it."

"Well, I'm glad you don't care, but let's just chill until the parking lot clears out a little more."

"How about we go to Llano and get a drink or something? I want to spend more time with you, and since it's officially spring break, I don't want to go home yet," Aaron suggests.

"K. Let me double check with Mom and make sure she doesn't care," I say, and then call Mom to ask. She tells me she doesn't mind, as long as we are back by midnight. *Yay!*

We switch places so Aaron can drive. I like it better when he drives, even though we are in my car. I'm hoping he will just tell me why he was late so that I don't have to ask him again. I don't want to make him mad and bug him about it, but I can't stop thinking about it. Finally, about half-way to town, I ask, "So, where were you earlier? I thought you were going to be there early and help me before the movie."

Aaron sighs, "Babe, I was just a little late. No big deal. We're together now, aren't we?"

What the crap? Why isn't he just telling me where he was?

"Yeah, and I'm glad we are together now. I just get worried," I say, as I look out my window. The rest of the ride is quiet. When we get to McDonald's, Aaron says he wants to go inside and get some food because he didn't have dinner.

"Sounds good. I could get another Happy Meal," I reply, remembering our being silly with my last Happy Meal toy. "I hope I get something awesome again," I say, smiling.

"You know you will! McDonald's toys are sweet!" We both laugh.

Once inside, we sit in the back corner so we will have a little privacy. Aaron gets three McDoubles and a large order of fries. I do not know how that boy can eat so stinkin' much, and I tease him as he scarfs it down. "Ummm, what the heck dude? You act like you haven't eaten all day, or maybe all week."

"Did you *see* what we had for lunch today? Freakin' disgusting!"

"Yeah, it was pretty much one of the cafeteria's worst creations," I smile, thinking about their version of Chinese food. I'm never brave enough to eat that, but I did have a snack after school, so I guess I wasn't as starving as him tonight. I don't think I could eat as much as him even if I was starving, though, and I tell him that while his mouth is full of French fries.

"I love you, ya big dork, even when you have French fries hanging out of your mouth!"

He shoves another huge bite into his mouth and says, "I lub you, too, sexthy!" He cracks me up and I throw a french fry at him.

~~~~~~~

We are taking Mom's suburban to Dallas. Dad is driving with Mom up front. Jamie, Carla, Aaron, and I are in the back and middle seats. Lily went with her best friend's family to San Antonio, so she isn't with us.

None of our parents were OK with us going to Dallas without adult supervision since we would be staying at a hotel, so Mom and Dad decided to chaperone us. Thankfully, we are all cool with it, though, because my parents are pretty good about giving us a lot of freedom to be silly and have fun. The concert isn't until Saturday night, so we are driving down on Wednesday and planning to go to Six Flags on Friday. On Thursday, we are just going to hang out at the hotel and swim during the day, and then we are going to eat out that night. It's all going to be so, so fun.

The guys keep making fun of Carla and me, though, because we have to stop for the bathroom in like every other town. I guess it's a girl thing, even though Aaron says *maybe* it's because I keep getting a new, giant Diet Dr.Pepper at every stop. I love having a drink and candy on road trips. It's like it's part of the trip fun for me. I figure it is kind of nice for everyone to stretch their legs every couple of hours anyway. In Sweetwater, we stop at a truck stop, and they have all kinds of weird Texas souvenirs. They have things made out of rattlesnake skin and even the rattlesnake heads on keychains. I tease Aaron, "You want one of those rattlesnake wallets, don't you, Aaron?"

He chuckles, replying, "You know I do! I want it to match the purse you want." Then Jamie notices a flyer for the Rattlesnake Roundup that is actually happening this weekend.

"Dude! We should totally stop by and check out the rattlesnakes on our way back from Dallas. I've heard about it but haven't ever been," Jamie tells us. Carla and I cringe, but Aaron seems to actually think it sounds like fun. I tell them they will have to clear that with my parents themselves if they want to go so badly, laughing. Apparently, they really do plan to ask if we can stop there on the way home Sunday.

We arrive at the hotel about four hours later. I am so not used to driving through the kind of traffic they have in Dallas and Fort Worth. It's kind of cool to experience it, but I don't think I could handle living here and driving in it all the time, and I am seriously happy that Dad is with us and he's driving.

The hotel is nice. We have adjoining rooms, so the boys are in the room next to the girls. It's kind of fun for Mom to be in our room and Dad to be in the guys' room. We can keep the door in between the rooms open until night time, or unless we are getting dressed, so it works out well.

We order pizza and play a couple of games that we brought with us for the rest of the night. *I can't believe I'm in Dallas with my best friend and our boyfriends. This is so awesome!*

~~~~~~~~

Six Flags was super fun, but some of the rides were crazy scary! Oh my gosh! I'm so glad I didn't get sick on some of those roller coasters. It would have been pretty embarrassing with Aaron sitting next to me on every ride. On one of them, after the ride, we could look at a picture they took of us while we were going down a really scary part, and we looked so hilarious! I was obviously screaming and my hair was all crazy, blowing around my face. Aaron looked like he was cracking up. Carla was covering her eyes in her picture, so that was funny. Mom and Dad actually rode it, too, and they both had their hands up and were smiling like they were having the best time of their lives. My parents are goofballs.

We are about to leave for the concert now. We have been getting ready with the door in between the rooms shut. Carla and I want to surprise the boys with our cute 80's looks. We didn't exactly tell them what we were planning. Stepping out into the hall at the same time, we crack up when we see that the boys sort of had the same idea. They have the shirts on that we gave them, but they ripped the sleeves off. Plus, they have eyeliner on, ripped jeans, bandannas around their heads, and they actually pierced their ears! I cannot even believe it, but it actually looks pretty hot, so I'm cool with it.

As we walk down the hall to the elevator, Aaron whispers to me, "Dang, babe! You look freakin' hot tonight!"

I smile and whisper back, "So do you! I can't believe you pierced your ears for this; you are so crazy, but I actually kind of love it." He chuckles and we head to the car.

The huge arena for the concert isn't very far from our hotel. Mom and Dad are dropping us off and going out on their own tonight. Handing our tickets to the people wearing yellow vests, we each walk through the turnstile and make our way through the crowd to Section 208, where our seats are together on the 1st row. It's cool because there is a metal railing in front of us, which actually makes it easier to see the stage than if people were sitting directly in front of us. I think we have a little more leg room, too. It's really loud already just with all of the people talking before the concert, and of course there is background music playing. There are a couple of opening bands that will play before Aerosmith, one that is apparently a local group on its way to making it big, and after that, Slash, the beast guitar player who used to be in Guns N' Roses. *Ummm, can you say, AWESOME? Woohoo!!!*

During the break, before Steven Tyler makes his appearance, we all head to the bathroom and also grab drinks. I'm dying of thirst after screaming and dancing, and we haven't even gotten to the main part yet. My hair is falling a little, but it still looks pretty cute. I have to wipe under my eyes to fix the smeared eyeliner when I see in the mirror that I am starting to look more like a zombie than a rocker girl.

Settled back in our seats just in time, the lights go off and the stage lights up dimly in red and blue with heavy fog. The crowd is screaming in anticipation, and all of a sudden the whole band is coming out one by one, a huge Aerosmith sign lighting up behind them. Steven Tyler is spotlighted as he sings into a microphone with a long scarf tied to it. The first song is one of their older ones and I don't know it very well, but it is still so cool that he is playing right in front of us. I really can't believe that this dude is like 66 years old and he can still sing and perform like this. He is SO good.

I turn my head to look at Aaron and he squeezes my hand when they play "I Don't Want To Miss A Thing." I love that song. Aaron stares into my eyes, singing along.

Wow! I almost feel like this is all too good to be true. I'm so happy, but I feel worried that it can't last like this.

Aerosmith closed with "Walk This Way," but then came back out for an encore singing, "Dream On." The high note in that song is ridiculous, and that song makes for a great ending to pretty much the most awesome night I've ever had in my life!

~~~~~~~~

We did end up stopping again in Sweetwater on the way home Sunday. I'm not sure how I would describe the Rattlesnake Roundup. It was fun, but it was bizarre and creepy to be so close to so many poisonous snakes. There was this guy who got into a big pit with so many snakes that they were up past his ankles. He had a stick thing and messed with some of them, which totally freaked me out. I'm pretty sure I would be just fine never seeing a rattlesnake in person again. It definitely made me glad I've never actually seen one out on our farm. I don't think all of the backing-away-slowly practice that I did when I was a kid could ever really prepare me for hearing that rattle sound and seeing a coiled up snake, staring at me with its evil-looking eyes. *Yuck!* However, despite their creepiness, we still got souvenirs, because I mean, really, how could we not? It is just too weird of a place to not get something to help us remember it. I just got a magnet though. I didn't really want anything made out of snake. Aaron and Jamie both got rattlesnake head key chains and teased Carla and me the rest of the way home. *Ugh! Why do boys love to be annoying?*

Chapter 13
April

Aaron's birthday is April 1st, which is a Wednesday. I know he's been teased at school all day since it is also April Fool's Day, which is kind of funny. I wanted to have a huge party for him but he insisted that he just wanted to hang out tonight, on his actual birthday, and not wait until the weekend. Dad is cooking steaks on the grill and Mom put some baked potatoes in the oven. It's kind of weird to have this particular meal during the middle of the week since we usually grill more on weekends, but I refuse to do nothing for Aaron's 18th birthday. To me, this one should definitely be celebrated. He's officially an adult in lots of ways; he can even vote. I made the cake right after school so that Aaron can blow candles out when we are finished with dinner. He told me once that he loves strawberries, so I am making a strawberry cake, another of my Grandma's delicious recipes. It's gooey and so yummy.

Aaron is outside with Dad while he is grilling, and I am setting the table. I expect his family to arrive any minute, and I also invited Carla and Jamie. I know he didn't want a giant party, but they are our best friends. Luckily, our table can be extended so that everyone can fit around it.

When everyone is here, Aaron seems happy to have all of us with him to celebrate, and he doesn't even seem to mind the balloons and banner I used to decorate the dining room. We all hold hands while Dad prays over the meal, and then everyone is fixing baked potatoes and cutting into the best steak around.

After singing to Aaron and watching him blow out 18 candles, we eat cake while telling him to hurry so he can open his presents, which he does. He eats his piece in three giant bites and laughs, saying, "I plan on having more after the presents. This cake is dee-lish!" Everyone around the table agrees about the cake and thanks me for making it. Grandma's recipes never fail.

Jamie and Carla got him the blue-ray discs of all of the Walking Dead series. My parents and I gave Aaron an Academy gift card because Aaron has been working out a lot lately.

"Thanks babe," Aaron says, kissing me lightly in front of everyone.

"You're welcome. I know it's not very personal, but I was thinking that this way, you could pick out some of the things you need or have been wanting."

The last present is from his family, and Aaron is surprised that they got him an IPad. They said they were thinking it would be a good thing to have in college next year, but something he could also go ahead and use now. Aaron hugs and kisses his parents, and before he can give his little brother a five, his brother is already asking to borrow it. Everyone laughs, when Aaron tells him, "Not in a million years little bro!" I think their track record for breaking his stuff is too high.

Aaron finally has to leave at 11 since it's a school night. I walk him to his truck and give him a kiss.

"I hope you had a good birthday."

"It was really great, Mia. It means a lot to me that you went to so much trouble. I really didn't expect anything big, ya know."

"Babe, you only turn 18 once, and you deserve it!" I tell him, giving him a huge hug. I quietly add, "I really love you, Aaron. I want to celebrate our birthdays together even when we are 100."

He chuckles, "That will be a fun one; we will be partying with our walkers and dancing while sitting in our chairs." I giggle, imagining us in the future, still in love and still having fun.

I had no idea how things were fixing to change dramatically.

~~~~~~~

Aaron wasn't at school on Friday, and he didn't answer my texts. By Saturday, I tried calling his Mom to make sure he was ok, and she said he had spent the night with Jamie. *That's weird. I wouldn't think he would be able to spend the night with Jamie after missing school. Jamie didn't mention it either.*

I texted Jamie, and he hadn't heard from Aaron.

I'm trying to decide whether or not to tell my parents. It's Saturday night, and I still haven't been able to get hold of Aaron, and Carla and I have been texting back and forth all day. I'm going to go hang out with her tonight, and probably spend the night. Maybe Jamie will meet up with us, and we can try to figure something out.

That's it. This is getting ridiculous. I'm telling Carla and Jamie about Aaron's situation. Maybe they can help me find him. I'm seriously freaking out.

At Carla's house, before we head over to pick Jamie up, I finally tell her.

"Sooo, I haven't told you this because Aaron asked me not to, but I'm really worried and I have to tell someone," I begin.

"What? What haven't you told me, Mia? You're scaring me a little here."

"It's just that, Aaron's parents…well, they adopted him a couple of years ago, and he's recently been in touch with his biological mom. She's crazy, Carla, and I'm afraid she could have something to do with Aaron being gone."

"Are you serious? But, he even looks like them. What the heck?…Why is this such a big secret anyway? It's not like we would be mean to him about it or anything," Carla says.

"I know. That's what Mom said. He really does fit in with their family so well, especially with his brown hair and eyes. Anyway, he was just embarrassed and he also worried because he made contact with his bio mom, and then she actually found him. He didn't want his parents to know because they worry so much," I explain. "Remember that night we were at Sonic, when we were first starting to hang out with Aaron?"

"Yeah, why?"

"Well, remember that crazy lady who knocked on our window? That was Aaron's bio mom!"

"No way! How weird. Why didn't he talk to her? Well, I guess I could see why…she looked kind of scary and messed up," Carla adds.

"I know. So anyway, I've actually met her now. We went to her house, and he loaned her money. She really didn't seem very nice or loving to him, but he still loves her. I'm trying really hard to understand it all, but it's hard, ya know?" I need Carla's reassurance. I don't know how to feel right now and I really need to talk this out with someone I trust, and I do trust Carla. We've been friends forever, and I know she wouldn't tell anyone.

"You MET her? You went to her house??? Are you crazy, Mia? That lady looked bad.   I mean, I know Aaron would protect you and everything, but that seems kind of risky."

"I know, but what else could I do? It's not like I would turn Aaron down when he asked me to meet her. Let's just hurry and get Jamie and tell him about it and see what he thinks. Maybe he will have an idea of how to find Aaron."

Jamie is waiting outside for us when we get to his house to pick him up. We had texted him to let him know we were on the way. As soon as he gets in the car, Carla looks at him and asks, "Hey, did you know Aaron was adopted?" Jamie looks a little nervous, and nods his head yes.

"WHAT?" Carla yells. "Why didn't you tell me? What the heck, Jamie? What all do you know?"

Jamie just tells us he knows that Aaron's bio mom has been around some, sort of stalking him. He explained that Aaron told him not to tell anyone, and he didn't even know that I knew. *Ugh! All these secrets are frustrating me. I hate this.*

Carla is still mad, and Jamie is telling her to just chill.

I finally say, "Ok y'all. We HAVE to find him. I think I can get us to his bio mom's house. Will y'all go with me?"

Carla asks, "Do you think it's safe? Shouldn't we talk to our parents or something?"

"What? No! We can't get him in trouble. We have to find him. I really need to know that he's ok. Please y'all? Let's just drive to Crockett and go to her house and see if his truck is there." Then I turn to Jamie, "You know the Alexanders think he's still with you, right? We have got to do this." I know I'm starting to sound a little crazy, but I just can't let this go. If we don't find him tonight, I don't know what I'll do. I guess I'll tell my parents, and they can talk to the Alexanders.

Please God, please help us find Aaron, and please keep us safe.

I went down the wrong road at first, but after driving down several of the roads in the neighborhood where Aaron's bio mom lives, I immediately spot the dilapidated house that still shocks me.

"That is the one, right there," I tell Jamie and Carla, pointing at the dark, broken-down house with beer cans littering the front steps. Aaron's truck is not here, but I feel like we should knock and check if his bio mom is home and if she has seen him lately. I'm definitely nervous, though.

"Ok, y'all come with me. Let's just knock and see if anyone answers and if his bio mom is there, maybe she will have seen him," I bravely suggest to Jamie and Carla.

They look at me wide-eyed like I'm insane but nod their heads, agreeing to be brave with me.

"What's the worst that can happen, right?" I ask them, leaving the answer up in the air.

We walk together down the crumbling sidewalk, using my cell phone flashlight to better light our path.

"You do it, Jamie," I tell him, pushing him ahead of Carla and me.

"Fine. I'm not afraid to knock on a door. Y'all are being rather wimpy if you ask me," Jamie says, puffing his chest out like he's some kind of big man.

Jamie knocks, and we wait, shivering and kind of huddled together because it's chilly tonight. We can hear someone in the house, and then all of a sudden the door opens, and Aaron is standing there just inside the door, seemingly surprised to see us.

He asks, "What are y'all doing here?"

He's looking at me, and I can't tell if he's mad or happy to see us, so I speak up, "Ummm, well, we haven't heard from you, and I kept trying to call and text you, and your mom said you were with

Jamie, but obviously you aren't, since he's with us. What's going on? Where's your truck?"

"Come in; it's too cold to keep the door open," he says, not yet answering any of my questions.

Carla and I sit on the old couch, and Jamie sits on the chair, while Aaron continues to stand up.

"Y'all want water or anything?" he asks.

I just shake my head, and I think I hear the others comment, "I'm good," and, "no thanks."

"So, what is going on? Why haven't you answered my calls or let me know where you are? I was getting really worried," I ask again.

"Everything is fine, babe. You're freakin' out over nothing. I just came to see my bio mom, and my phone died, and I forgot my charger," he reassures me.

"Well, then where is your truck? How did you get here?"

"Oh, yeah, Mom needed to borrow it last night to go to work because she said she was running late and didn't have time to catch the bus; she just hasn't gotten back yet. I'm sure she will be here soon. I told her I planned to go back home tonight."

Jamie shakes his head, saying, "Dude! Your mom thinks you are with me. What if she found out? Are you sure it's really a great idea to let your bio mom borrow your truck? I mean, seriously, you told me about some of the things she has done in the past, and it just seems a little crazy to me."

"Well nobody freakin' asked you, did they?" Aaron answers defensively. "I think I know her better than you do, and I'm 18 years old now. I am perfectly capable of making decisions about who uses my truck and where I stay the night."

"Chill, man. I'm not trying to upset you. It's just that, like Mia said, we didn't know where you were, and we were all kind of getting concerned. Forget I said anything," Jamie says, trying to calm Aaron down.

The whole room reeks of smoke, and I notice an open pack of cigarettes on the table. If she hasn't been here since last night, then I can only assume Aaron has been smoking.

"I didn't know you smoked, Aaron." I say, feeling like I don't know him as well as I thought I did. I'm really frustrated. If he loves me and we are close, he should have told me about his plans to do this. He has to know I would have been worried if I hadn't heard from him in a couple of days.

Aaron looks down and answers, "It's not a big deal, Mia. I just smoked a few of Mom's. I used to do it, and it had been a long time; crap, I first started when I was 9. She offered it to me, and I figured I would just do it a little while I'm here. I'm not gonna keep smoking around you, if that's what you're worried about."

I can feel my jaw drop. *Nine? What the heck? I can't even imagine a kid smoking that young.*

Ignoring his answer, I continue grilling him. I don't really mean to sound like some kind of mom or cop. I just have to know what he's thinking. I love him so much, but I just don't know if I can handle it if he is going to be doing weird stuff and not letting me know where he is half the time.

"So, have you done other drugs?" I realize it isn't probably the best time to ask him something like this, especially with our friends sitting here with us, but I need to know.

"What do *you* think, Mia? The crap was always available to me. Mom encouraged it, and sometimes, it was nice to just get away. I didn't do much, but I have tried a few things. Are you mad? I've told you before that my past was bad. I knew this crap would happen. It was just a matter of time before you decided you couldn't deal with who I am."

"Really, Aaron? Because I feel like I've been very understanding and encouraging. I've told you a million times, I'm not worried about your past. I'm worried about your future, *our* future," I say, feeling upset. I add, "I mean, what am I supposed to think right now, Aaron? I came and found you, and thank God you are fine, but here you are smoking and acting like everything is fine and that this is just who you are and that I'm being stupid. I don't know how I'm supposed to feel right now," I say, as I get up, feeling very ready to leave and head back to the comfort of our tiny town.

"So that's it? You're leaving? This is who I am, Mia. I know my bio mom may not be the most perfect person, but she's trying. I only kept it from my family because I really don't want the hassle of them getting all freaked out about me seeing her. I know what I'm doing, and I'm not doing anything wrong."

"I'll just talk to you later, Aaron. I need some time to think. Come on, y'all," I say to Carla and Jamie.

Jamie shakes Aaron's hand and tells him, "Dude, just give her some time. I'm sure it will all be fine. Be careful, though, man, and let me know when you get home so we can talk more."

I look at Aaron, feeling very sad that we are fighting and that I'm leaving without making up. Before I can get to the truck, though, he grabs me into a hug and says, "It'll be fine, Mia. I'm still the same person. I'll call you later." I hug him back, not sure if this will be the last time. Everything just feels different.

~~~~~~~

I guess Aaron's bio mom made it back with his truck because he's with his family at church this morning. They aren't sitting with us, though, and he hasn't talked to me. I feel like I really need worship this morning; it always makes me feel closer to God, and I love praising Him. I close my eyes so that I won't be distracted, and I let go and sing. We are singing *Oceans* by Hillsong, and I feel like God is speaking to me through the lyrics as I sing along about the spirit of God leading me and making my faith stronger.

I know that I have to trust in God, that He will guide me, and I do feel like I trust Him. I just don't see the direction He wants me to go yet. Do I continue to try to encourage and love Aaron through his problems, or do I stay away so that I am not possibly put in a bad situation?

After church, and for the rest of the day, I don't hear from Aaron. He doesn't show up at youth, and I feel disappointed, but it gives me an opportunity to talk to Kathy. I pull her aside after most everyone leaves, and she asks me what's up.

"So, Aaron has been hanging out with his bio mom more lately. He went to her house, spent the night, and even loaned her his truck. He told his family that he was spending the night with Jamie, and we couldn't get a hold of him, so Jamie, Carla, and I decided to go to his bio mom's house and see if we could find him. He was there by himself, and he was smoking. He said he has tried drugs in the past, too. He seemed mad and defensive, though, when we asked him about it. I just don't know what to do, Kathy. I love him, but I'm nervous about where he's headed if he keeps associating with her. What do you think?"

"Well, I think it sounds like he is still struggling with finding his identity. He just turned 18, right?" she asks.

"Yes."

"I know that Kenny mentioned that birthdays could be difficult for him because it was a milestone that his bio family was missing. I would think that turning 18, an age that is looked at as adulthood in many ways, would be even more significant to him.

Maybe he was seeking his bio mom's love, or maybe he feels like he *is* an adult and, therefore, he can be more independent."

"Hmmm, I didn't think about the birthday issue. I wonder if she acknowledged his birthday," I say, thinking how awful it would be if she forgot It.

"The thing is, Mia, that Aaron is still learning who he is. He is looking for direction, probably feeling torn between his identity now with his adopted family and his previous identity with his bio family. We have to continue to pray that he will recognize his true identity in God, because, ultimately, that is all that matters. Just keep praying for him, Mia, and we will as well. God is bigger than this, and He is in control."

"But what if Aaron starts hanging around his bio mom all the time. How long do I keep encouraging him and waiting for him to choose the right path? I don't believe his bio mom is good for him, and I'm just afraid he will embrace that life instead of all of the good things his adopted family has for him, and of course, what God has for him," I say, feeling teary.

"I can't tell you how long you should continue a dating relationship with Aaron, but even if you choose to break up with him, I hope you will try to be his friend. He needs positive people in his life, and like I said, you can still always pray for him, whatever your relationship is," Kathy smiles, encouraging me.

"Thanks, Kathy. I'm so glad I can talk to you about this. I haven't talked much to my parents about it, and it helps to have an adult's point of view."

"No problem, Mia. You know you can talk to me anytime. Just remember, Aaron's bio mom needs prayer, too. Even though she may continue to struggle with her own issues, Aaron loves her, and so does God, so you can't think of *her* as the wrong path, but rather, the bad lifestyle she is leading as the wrong path."

Dear God,

Please help Aaron discover himself without going in the wrong direction. Please protect him and guide him and help me to know how I can help him. Lord, please also guide me. I don't know what my part is in this. I need You, God. I just want to be close to You. I want to do Your will. I love You, God. Thank You for all of my blessings, Lord.

Sometimes I realize I ramble when I talk to God, but I know He knows what I mean. *It's a good thing since I don't even always know what I really want to say.*

~~~~~~~

It's been a week, and I still haven't talked much to Aaron. We have texted back and forth, and I saw him at school, but he left every day pretty quickly after school let out. Every time we talked, it was pretty much like nothing happened, like everything is the same as it was before last weekend. It's Friday, though, so before he can get away, I catch him at his truck right after school.

"Babe, wait!" I say, running up to his window.

"Hey sexy, what's up?" Aaron asks me, smiling.

I smile and feel myself flush at his calling me "sexy," but it's a little odd because we haven't talked in forever, and he keeps acting like nothing is different.

"Ummm, well, I was just seeing what you are doing. I feel like we haven't really hung out in a while and I miss you," I answer.

"I know. I'm sorry; I miss you, too. I have something I need to do tonight, but let's go out tomorrow. I will take you to a movie or something," he says, but he seems like his mind is on something else.

"Ok, I'll just wait to hear from you tomorrow then, I guess," I say, and then walk away towards my car.

"Bye, babe!" he yells out the window while already backing up out of his parking spot. I don't even turn around as I say quietly, pretty much just to myself, "bye."

Carla and I decide we should use this as a movie night with each other at her house, so I am spending the night with her. Doing this feels like a comfort to me, which I really need right now. We are planning on watching movies and then doing each other's nails. I don't really do much with my nails because every time I paint them, it seems like they start peeling within a day, and then my OCD takes over and I start messing with them, picking the rest of the polish off, one fingernail at a time. I decided a long time ago that it is easier and actually looks better if I just try to leave them alone and go *au naturale*. I am letting Carla paint my toenails, though, and she is doing each one a different color.

"I sure am rockin' this rainbow toe look, huh Carla!" I tell her, laughing and putting my feet up to look at both at the same time.

"They look AWESOME, dude! Of course, what else would you expect from a professional like me?" she jokes back.

It feels good to laugh and be silly. I have missed hanging out with my best friend. It's like, I want to grow up and have a boyfriend and do new things, but this is really making me realize that there was nothing wrong with the innocence and simplicity of how things have always been before my life became a little more complicated. Unfortunately, that thought makes me sad, though, because it makes me remember my current situation, despite my trying to escape it all night.

"Carla, I don't know what is gonna happen with Aaron. He said he would see me tomorrow, but he rushed off today after school *again*. What the heck is going on with him? It's like he's changing, and I am not sure I'm liking the new him. I feel guilty even thinking that way, but gosh, what the crap am I supposed to think?" I confide.

"I don't know, Mia. Jamie hasn't really hung out with Aaron, either, so I don't know anything more than you do, but I understand how you feel. He's definitely being weird."

I hug the fluffy pink pillow that I brought with me, continuing to look at my feet. "I know. Weird, distant, different. Do you think he doesn't want his life here, like, with the Alexanders, and also with me?" I ask her, hoping she won't confirm my biggest fear.

"I don't know what he wants, Mia, but I don't think any of this means he doesn't still want to be with you. I mean, don't you think he would have told you if he wanted to break up or something?" she asks.

"What if he is seeing someone else, like from his past?" I say worriedly, and the tears start to fall, as they have several times lately.

Carla comes to hug me and reassure me, "Don't go there, Mia. Just talk to him tomorrow and ask him what his deal is. Tell him you feel worried. Just be honest with him; I know it will make you feel better. Don't think about it anymore tonight. Let's go to the kitchen and see if we have any ice cream," she says, pulling me to my feet.

"Fine. I will try my hardest," I say, knowing it will not be easy for me.

~~~~~~~~

I have decided that I'm not going to text or call Aaron first today. He said he would see me today, but I don't know what his plans are, and since he's been kind of distant lately, I will just wait until he contacts me. I can't help checking my phone repeatedly throughout the day, though.

Finally, around 5:00, I get a text:

"Hey babe! WRUD?"

"Nothing really. How about u?" I reply.

"I've been helping Dad with stuff around the house, but I'm fixin' 2 go 2 Crockett. Wanna come with?"

Ummmm, hello? Did he forget he was planning to take me to a movie or something?

"What r u doing in town?" I text back.

"Just an errand. I'll come get u."

"K. See u in a sec."

I'm definitely feeling a little uneasy with the way he's not being very open right now, but I do want to see him. I miss him so badly. I miss his normal self, anyway. I wonder if the Aaron I know is the real him, or if there is another side of him that I don't know at all. While waiting, I take a picture of my crossed feet as I sit on my front porch. It's actually a pretty decent day, so I can wait outside. I love it so much when it finally starts getting warm enough to be outside without either freezing to death or it being so windy that dirt gets in my mouth and eyes. I post the picture on Instagram with the caption, "Waiting to head to town with my handsome boy!" I tag Aaron and add three pink hearts. Maybe if I act normal, I can convince myself that everything else is normal, including Aaron.

Aaron turns down my little road leading to the house, so I head over to meet him. I smile as I jump into the truck and give him a quick kiss before getting buckled.

"Hi!" I say, maybe a little over-enthusiastically.

He smiles back. "Hey babe! Are you happy to see me or what?"

"What do you think, dork?"

"I think you better be happy to see me. Come here," he replies, pulling me even closer than I already am.

"I can't exactly sit on your lap while you are driving, ya know," I tease, giggling.

"Well, you can at least sit as closely as possible."

He scoops my hand up in his and intertwines our fingers as they rest together on my leg, while using his left hand to drive. *This is good. This is right.*

On the outskirts of town I ask him again, "So, what's the plan?"

"I need to pick something up at my mom's and then we can go walk around the mall or something. Is that cool with you?"

"Sure. What are you picking up?" I ask, hoping he will open up to me more.

"I'm not sure; she just asked me to come by because she has something for me."

"Have you seen her a lot lately?"

"I don't know, maybe two or three times in the last couple of months? Why?" he asks.

"I just wondered." I don't want him to be mad at me for asking but I'm still trying to figure out what the deal is.

"Everything's fine, Mia. Mom has been better, so there's nothing to worry about. K?" He picks up our entwined hands and turns them so that he can kiss my hand. My heart swells. *Man, I really love him so much.*

When we pull up to his mom's house, there is a faded, old trans-am sitting crookedly in the driveway. I glance over at Aaron and notice his face looks angry, confused, worried. He quickly parks and jumps out of the truck, telling me to wait in the cab. I try to ask him what is going on, but he is shutting the door and jogging up to the door before I can even get the words out.

I feel very nervous and anxious as I watch him knock on the door several times before it finally opens. He all of a sudden goes still when a man opens the door, and steps out, closing the door behind him but standing in between the door and Aaron. Aaron takes maybe one step back, but yells, "What are you doing here?"

The man is a little taller than Aaron, and he seems intimidating and looks like he's lived a hard and rough life. His arms are covered in tattoos and his hair is pulled back into a low pony tail with a long, unshaped beard covering the front of his face. It looks like he even has tattoos on his face, making it hard to really see what he looks like. He has his hands on his hips and continues to tower over Aaron, but Aaron doesn't seem fazed, his own anger taking over as he continues yelling at the man, telling him to get out of the way so that Aaron can go in and see his mom. I notice the man look over at me, and when Aaron notices, I see him close in, threatening the man, who just chuckles and starts to head towards me. I'm trying to decide if I have time to call someone for help, but I don't want to appear rude, in case I'm getting freaked out over nothing. When he opens the door, Aaron tries to stop him, but the man easily pushes him aside. Aaron looks at me, and I see concern mixed with embarrassment and disgust in his eyes, but I don't have time to think much about it before it registers that the man is talking to me.

"Who might you be, pretty girl? Why don't you get out and let me get a better look at you?"

Cringing, I sit still, hoping he's not serious. His eyes become fierce, and he lowers his voice, "I said, get out of the truck. No need to be afraid. I just want to get to know the girl my son brought home. He seems to think he can keep you all to himself."

Oh my gosh. Please God, help us NOW!

I slowly get out of the truck, keeping my eyes on Aaron, hoping for some sort of reassurance that I don't need to really be scared, that this is just a bluff or a front. I can't believe this man is Aaron's father. He seems very scary, and maybe a little crazy.

"Now then, let's all head into the house so we can visit. I haven't seen my son in a long time, and I think it's about time we get reacquainted."

Aaron's father leads us up the porch and into the house, where it is dimly lit. I have to let my eyes readjust just so I can see, when I notice Aaron's mom laying on the couch. She appears to be asleep, or passed out; I can't tell. Aaron rushes to her and shakes her, "Mom! Mom! Are you ok?"

She keeps her eyes closed, but smiles, and slurs, "Aaron! I'm so glad you're here. Did you see your surprise? Your father is here to see you." She kind of lifts one hand, motioning toward Aaron's dad, like this is a good thing. *They are both crazy. I seriously do NOT want to be here!*

Aaron's dad tells her to move so we can sit on the couch, and when she doesn't do it quickly, he walks over and shoves her off of the couch, causing her to hit the floor with a thud. Aaron starts to say something, but before he can, his dad puts his hand up, telling him with one little gesture to be quiet. I'm thankful nobody noticed me jump when she fell. I mean, it's not like she could really get hurt falling such a short distance, but it shocked me to see him be so rough with her. I realize I still don't even know Aaron's dad's name, so I try to introduce myself, hoping we can change the mood, which would definitely put me more at ease.

"It's good to meet you finally, sir. I'm Mia," I say, hoping he doesn't notice the shake in my voice.

He turns his attention to me, answering, "What? Did Aaron not tell you about me?" while glancing back and forth between Aaron and me.

Ignoring the question, I try again, "I'm sorry, sir, but what is your name?"

He grunts, "You can call me Dad, just like Aaron does."

Oh God. I wince, thinking there is no way in crap that I'm going to be calling this man, "Dad."

Thankfully, Aaron keeps his eyes down, but says to me, "His name is Dean. You can call him Dean."

I just nod my head; obviously, I am not helping things with this conversation. Before there can be too much awkward, or maybe I should say, creepy silence, Aaron's mom chimes in, "So, *Dean,*" emphasizing his name like she's trying to be funny or something, "tell Aaron what you told me." She is sitting up on the floor with her back leaning against the couch, eyes half open, but apparently alert enough to follow the conversation.

Aaron looks at him, expectantly, and I'm hoping whatever he has to say isn't any more shocking than this whole little reunion has already been.

Dean looks at Aaron and grins, "I'm back for good, kid. Now, you can come back and live here with us, too. You need to help out around here."

Aaron looks so angry, but I'm sure he is trying to think of the right thing to say just to get us out of here for now. He's hesitating too long, I think, and Dean is just staring right at him, waiting him out. Dean then acts like he realizes what the problem is, "Oh, of course Mia can come over anytime, too. In fact, she could probably be pretty useful around here as well."

That's when Aaron moves to stand in between his dad and me, protectively. "She won't be coming here again; I was just giving her a ride to her house, but she's just a friend. In fact, I need to get her home and then I'll be right back."

Surely this is an act to get us out of here.

Before we can get very close to the door, though, Dean says, "Oh, let me. I was about to head to the store to get more to drink anyway. How 'bout it pretty girl? Where can I take you?"

"Oh, uh, that's ok sir, Aaron knows the way, and I can just wait to go with him." I smile, though, trying to stay calm.

"Alright, but next time, you and I are gonna get to know each other a little better. I'll be right back," but he warns Aaron first. "You better be here when I get back. I don't want to have to come looking for you, or your pretty, little *friend* here." He smiles at me and saunters out the door. I hear the car rev its engine before backing up and squealing off down the road. Aaron and I have been still, feeling the shock of what just happened and waiting until it feels safe to move.

I grab Aaron quickly, "Babe, I think we need to go now. Let's go, ok?" Aaron is just standing there, though, in disbelief, and I say it again, this time louder, "Come on! Let's go. I want to go home. Come on!" I pull his hand and try to get him to snap out of it, but when he does, he goes to his mom and kneels down in front of her.

"Mom. Mom!" He is struggling to get her to focus enough and pay attention.

"Did he hurt you? Why is he here, Mom? I thought you were done with him." Aaron hits the couch with his fist, furious.

His mom's mouth turns up, though, and she answers him, "Aaron, isn't it great? He's back, and things are going to be the way they used to be. I knew he would come back."

"What the hell, Mom? Why do you always do this crap? I hate him! And you know what? I freakin' hate you, too. You are so freaking stupid. We're leaving, and I WON'T be coming back. Y'all better leave us alone, too, or I will call the cops on you. You understand me, mom? It's me or him, and apparently you are choosing him, like you always did before."

He grabs me, "Let's go, Mia."

I have never felt more relieved as I did when we were back in the truck, driving back towards Coyote, to safety. Aaron quietly said he was sorry when we first got back in the truck, but after that, the rest of the drive was quiet. When he dropped me off at my house, I tried to talk to him, but he said he needed time to think, and then he left.

~~~~~~~

Two weeks later, the last week in April, and I haven't seen Aaron other than school. He refuses to talk to me. I've tried texting him, calling him, even just talking to him at school, but he ignores me or says I need to just give him more time.

I mean, how much time does he need? Why does he need time away from me anyway? I am beyond frustrated, even though obviously I still care about Aaron. He is not talking to any of his friends either, not even Jamle, and I haven't seen him at church for the last two weekends. I saw his mom at church last Sunday, though, so I decided to ask her how he is doing and why he hasn't been at church. She shrugged and said she thinks he is just going through some stuff right now and that she doesn't want to push him to go if he doesn't want to. She asked me how he's acted at school, and I wasn't sure how much she knows, so I told her he hasn't really talked to any of us lately. She didn't seem worried, so I'm guessing she doesn't know anything about the incident we had with his bio parents.

I haven't told anyone about that day except for Carla. I probably should have, but I felt like things were fine as long as we didn't go back to that house again. I guess "fine" is all relative because obviously Aaron is not "fine."

Since school is close to being out for summer, there are a lot of things going on, big things, like prom. Aaron hasn't talked to me, so I have no idea if he is even planning to go, and it's only a week away now. At our school, the juniors and seniors all get to go to prom, so I'm going, even if Aaron doesn't. I want him to go with me. This is my first prom, and I want it to be special, but I don't know what more I can do. If Aaron refuses to talk to me, I guess I will just leave him alone for now. It really sucks.

Carla and I already bought our dresses a month ago. I told Aaron when I bought my dress that it is pale yellow because usually the guy gets the same color accents on his tux. I have no idea if he ever even ordered his tux, though. *Ugh!*

I decide that since it's Saturday, I will drive over to Aaron's house, and make him talk to me, at least long enough to tell me if he is going to go to prom. If he doesn't want to talk more than that, fine. I'm sick of trying.

When I get there, I notice that Aaron's truck is gone, but his dad is outside and walking towards me as I pull up, so I turn the car off and get out to talk to him for a minute.

"Hi, Mia! How have you been?" he asks, warmly.

I smile. He's such a nice man. I wish Aaron would have never had to live with anyone before the Alexanders. I wish they were his real parents, or at least that he could see them that way.

"I've been ok. Thanks. How have you been, Mr. Alexander?"

"Doing well. So, I'm assuming you came here to see Aaron, but he isn't here right now. He got a job in town, so he's been working most nights after school and on weekends."

What? Why wouldn't he have told me that?

"Oh, well, he didn't tell me. That's weird. Where's he working?" I ask him.

"Hmm, I don't know why he wouldn't have told you either, but he's been working with a friend of his that he knew from Crockett who has his own business working on people's yards. The boy's name is Anthony. Have you met him?"

"No, sir. I haven't, but that's good I guess." I feel like once again, I am realizing there is more to Aaron than I know, and it's really upsetting.

"Yeah, this boy grew up in foster care and the state helped him get his business going somehow, so he asked Aaron if he wanted to help him. He's a good kid, responsible," Mr. Alexander says.

"Ok. Well, will you have him call me when he gets home? I need to talk to him about prom." He assures me he will, so I smile and jump back in my car to head home.

Alrighty then. Apparently, I don't even know my boyfriend very well. Lately, he hasn't even acted like a boyfriend to me, so who knows? Maybe he doesn't want to be with me anymore. I hate this.

Of course, as I expected, Aaron never called me. He's totally blowing me off, and I'm getting tired of it. I know he has issues, but the least he could do is talk to me. When I see him at school on Monday, I decide that if he wants to talk to me, he can, but I'm not talking to him. I'm mad. I know it's not right to play games, but I'm so done. I can just go by myself to prom. *When I'm being honest with myself, though, that sounds really un-fun.*

All week, we have ignored each other, and prom is tonight. I got up early, and Carla and I went to Crockett together to get our hair and makeup done. I'm determined to look super hot. If he even shows, he will not be able to ignore me anymore. That's for sure.

Thankfully, Carla and Jamie have let me ride with them, since prom is in town at a hotel. I really didn't want to drive to Crockett by myself while all fixed up. It just felt weird.

We all walk in together, and it looks so pretty. The theme is Midnight Masquerade and there are black and silver balloons and streamers decorating the room, with really pretty glasses on the tables that we get to keep after the night is over. Carla and I squeal in excitement. It feels so cool to be going to my first prom. I'm trying very hard to forget about the awful feeling in the back of my mind that Aaron isn't here sharing it with me.

We take pictures before the line gets too long, and then sit down to a catered Italian meal. It is delicious. Aaron is still not here, and I long to see him. Jamie hasn't heard from him, and he hasn't heard of the kid, Anthony, that apparently Aaron is working with.

As the night goes on, I try to lose myself and just have fun, dancing with my friends and being silly. There are about five other girls who don't have dates, so we all dance together and don't worry about how we look. At least I don't have the pressure of trying to dance well since I'm ridiculously awkward and uncoordinated.

After it's over, Jamie and Carla want to hang out, but I have them take me home first. Even though I had a good time, I pretty much want this night to be over.

Before I go to bed, my hair still curly spread out on my pillow, I decide I need to text Aaron.

"I missed you at prom tonight. You've finally made it clear enough to me. I will leave you alone. I really wish you the best. I hope you will stay in touch after high school. Love, Mia."

I wrote it more like a letter than a text, because it feels weird to write something so serious in text language. I even signed it so I would have one more chance to tell him I love him. This has been a very hard decision to make, but I feel like my heart can't handle anymore. Tears hit my pillow as I cry myself to sleep.

Chapter 14
May

"So, I told Aaron in a text that I'm breaking up with him," I tell Carla at school Monday.

"Are you serious? What did he say?" she asks, knowing how much I never thought I would be the one to break up. I am pretty sure he broke up first, though. He just didn't say it.

I really thought we would be together forever. I mean, like, I had my life mapped out in my head...after high school, I would go to college, and after that, I would marry Aaron and we would have a family and live happily ever after. Of course, I knew we would have minor issues along the way, but I truly believed we were meant for each other, and this feels so wrong to me, but I know it is the right thing to do. He left me a month ago. I just didn't want to believe it then.

"He didn't say anything. He hasn't talked to me in forever; why would he now?" I answer her, feeling defeated.

"Wow. I'm so sorry, Mia. Maybe y'all will get back together when things calm down for him. Maybe he's just still really freaked out about his dad coming back and everything," she tries to reassure me.

"Well, it's not exactly looking like that's going to happen. I've given him time, Carla. Plus, I found out he has a job that I didn't even know he had. I mean, what the heck? I feel like I never really knew him."

"Well, look at it this way. It's the end of the year, and we are going to be SENIORS next year! This is supposed to be the best time of our life, so let's just focus on you and all of the awesome things coming up for us!"

I nod and smile, trying so hard to believe everything is good. I'm not trying to convince Carla, though, as much as I am myself.

~~~~~~~

I feel like this month is going by so quickly. *Is it possible for me to have* Senioritis *when I'm only a Junior?* I am so done with this year. I really don't even care about the band concert coming up, or my finals, or anything for that matter. I feel a little like a zombie; I hope I don't actually look like one, though. I don't think *Walking Dead* would look very good on me. I've tried to focus on finishing out the year with all A's. So far, I have gotten A's in every class for every six weeks. I'm currently third in my class, but there is a boy who is competing with me for that spot big time. We are so close to each other, but the girls who are first and second are far enough ahead of us that we won't likely catch up with them. I don't really care. I feel like third in my class is pretty good, even if I do only have thirteen people in my class. Focusing on my grades has not been my priority this year. Even though I have done well, I'm sure I could have done even better. I have just been so distracted by Aaron and my social life. I can't say I regret it, but now that it's over, I realize that I probably shouldn't have let myself get so carried away.

My stupid science class is kind of kicking my butt this six weeks. I will freaking die if I get a B after having not gotten one all year, but I know I am right on the edge. I'm working on an extra credit project, since I seem to have a ton of time on my hands. I have to write a research paper on a recent science discovery. *Ugh.*

Like I really want to even read about anything science related, much less write about it.

It's due next week, so I've been working on it all weekend. I hear a soft knock at the door to my room, and Mom peeks her head in.

"Hey sweetie; can I come in?"

"Sure," I answer her, closing my laptop as I sit on my bed, leaning against a bunch of pillows that I have stacked along the wall. "What's up?"

"Nothing. I just wanted to check on you. You haven't really talked to me much since you and Aaron broke up. Are you doing ok? You seem pretty quiet lately."

"I'm ok, I guess," I say, even though I tear up anyway. I think there is something about getting sympathy from Mom that makes me extremely emotional. It's like she is somehow validating all of my feelings, and I feel sorry for myself, like my mind is thinking, "I know, right? My life really is horrible. I should be bawling my eyes out." *I know. I am such a freakin' dork.* I can't help it, though. The tears just start falling like crazy.

Mom comes and sits beside me on my bed and just hugs me.

"It's ok. You've been trying so hard to keep a brave face. It's ok to cry. I know how close you were to Aaron." She's trying to make me feel better, but I can't help but cry even more.

"You don't even know half of it, Mom."

"What does that mean, Mia?"

"I'm not sure I should talk about it."

"About what? You're scaring me a little, ya know."

"It's nothing you need to worry about, Mom. It's not like I've done anything bad," I say, knowing she is thinking the worst, like I'm pregnant or something.

"Ok. Well, then what is it? You know you can talk to me," she says.

"Ok, but you can't tell anyone." I hesitate, and then just let it all out. I tell her about Aaron having contact with his bio parents, and about my having gone to his mom's house. Then I tell her about Aaron's dad and the scary incident that led up to all of the crazy in my life. Her eyes are wide, and I can tell she's trying to remain calm, but she still says, "Mia! You should have never gone over there, especially without letting us know. What if something would have happened to you?"

"I know, Mom. I'm really sorry. I didn't think I was in danger or anything... until last time."

"I have to at least tell your father, and then I really think we need to let the Alexanders know. I know you didn't want me to say anything, but this is a big deal, Mia, especially since Aaron's dad was threatening y'all."

"Oh my gosh, Mom. What if they get mad at me for not telling them before? I definitely didn't want Aaron to get mad at me, but I guess now that we aren't even together, it doesn't really matter anymore," I say, worriedly. "Can we at least wait until school is out so I don't have to see him?"

"Let's talk to Dad and see what he thinks, but I really do think they need to know. This could potentially affect their whole family, but I bet it could wait until school is out. That's only one more week."

"Ok." That's the only response I can muster, since I'm not confident whether or not this is the right thing to do.

~~~~~~~

We took two cars to Crockett on Sunday. We are going to eat out after church, and then after that, Mom and I are going to go grocery shopping. Dad said he had to get back home early, but I bet he is just going to sneak in a nap. I definitely don't blame him for not wanting to go grocery shopping, though. I really don't love going. I can't help but organize everything in the basket, fitting it all together like a puzzle, another one of my lovely OCD traits. Since I'm feeling so out of control over everything in my life, I am worse than usual, and I keep moving things around to make them fit better. Lily is with us and she keeps rolling her eyes, and then just throws crap into the basket. It drives me insane! *Can she seriously not agree with me that the box of pop tarts fits in the corner of the basket by other boxes and that the frozen foods all go together? UGH!!!* I'm about to smack her when I notice some people at the end of the aisle.

"I can't believe it!" I say out loud but to myself. Mom looks up, "What, dear?" Then she follows my gaze to the end of the aisle where Aaron is walking with his bio dad. It's obvious to her that the man is Dean because I had described him when I told her all about how scary he is. Mom says, "Oh my." Lily asks what we are talking about, and I just tell her to shush. I don't exactly want to bring attention to myself. I probably am, though, since I am frozen, a bag in one hand and bananas in the other. I'm staring, and all of a sudden, Aaron makes eye contact with me. He stares back, hard, but when his dad says something, Aaron diverts him to another section of the store, leaving without any other contact.

Mom asks, "I thought he wasn't seeing them anymore, Mia?!"

"So did I, Mom," I say with the same exact tone as her.

Lily interrupts again, "What is going on?" louder this time.

"Chill. It doesn't concern you. *Gosh!*"

Mom corrects me, "Mia, there's no reason to be ugly to your sister. Lily, just don't worry about it. Everything is fine."

"Fine," she mutters, clearly disappointed that we are leaving her out of the situation. I just don't feel like going into all of it, and I don't think she needs to know everything anyway.

"Thank you," I say sarcastically, still being kind of a butt. I don't know what to think. I wonder if Aaron is with his dad by choice. *Did Dean find Aaron and blackmail him or something? Or did Aaron just want to be with his other family? I mean, clearly he's different now.*

~~~~~~~

I guess Mom decided that telling Dad and the Alexanders couldn't wait anymore because they are at our house, and Mom has called me into the room. We are sitting around the table, and they are anxiously waiting for me to tell them everything. I feel like such a jerk for keeping this all quiet. Thankfully, Aaron's parents are being very nice and telling me that it's not my fault but that I just need to tell them everything so that they can help Aaron.

What if I could have saved him from all of this just by telling someone a long time ago?

After everything is out in the open, the Alexanders thank me and my parents before leaving. Heading back to my room to finish the last little bits of my paper, I can't help worrying about Aaron.

> *Please God. Please let Aaron be OK. I'm so sorry that I didn't tell anyone about what's been going on. Please forgive me, God, and please help me to be brave tomorrow at school when I see him. In Jesus' Name, Amen.*

~~~~~~~

Aaron isn't at school Monday or even Tuesday. Finals are Wednesday and Thursday, so I briefly see him in passing in the halls as he makes his way to class. He makes eye contact, which he hasn't done in a long time during school. In fact, he's pretty much avoided me at all cost before now. I can't tell what he's thinking as he stares me as we pass each other in the hall. It's like an empty stare, no feeling at all behind his eyes. This scares me more than anger.

After school, I text Aaron and tell him I'm sorry, that I was just trying to do what I felt was right. He doesn't respond.

Friday is a half-day, and then graduation is at seven in the evening in the school auditorium. Aaron is graduating, so of course I will be there regardless of whether or not he wants me there. I have other friends graduating, so I can use that as an excuse.

The graduation ceremony in a small school is very unique. Since there aren't many students, the school finds a way to make it last forever anyway, which is kind of annoying, but I'm sure I might appreciate it more next year when it's my turn.

There is a guest speaker, speeches made by the valedictorian and salutatorian, and then the historian, who is the person third in the class, always shows a slide show of the history of the class. It's my favorite part, which is also why I hope to be third, because there are always funny pictures of all of the senior kids. They always have baby pictures and a couple of school pictures, and then discuss the various extracurricular things in which each student was involved, finally followed by a senior picture. Since there are twenty kids in this class, it isn't too big of a deal to do this for each student. Since Aaron joined the class late, he is towards the end of the presentation. There are no baby pictures of Aaron, and the only other ones are some that have been taken since he has attended this school. It makes me so incredibly sad. I wonder if his bio parents ever took pictures of him. Even if they did, I kind of doubt they still have them, and I'm sure they wouldn't share them with the Alexanders. I can see each kid sitting on the stage, and while most are smiling and totally excited about graduating, Aaron seems solemn.

After the ceremony is complete, the students form a receiving line in the cafeteria for a reception, and all of the guests go through the line congratulating them, one by one. Aaron is the first in line, so when it's my turn, I hug him and tell him congratulations. Surprisingly, he doesn't resist, and actually even hugs me back. He just says, "Thank you, Mia," into my hair, making me feel like I might die a little more because I don't want to let go. I have to, though, because there is a big line still behind me waiting for a turn to talk to the graduates. By the time the line has fizzled out, I don't see Aaron or his family. I wonder if they left early.

I feel so incredibly sad. What if that was the last time I will ever see Aaron again? I've never been so sad for summer to be here.

Chapter 15
June

I'm sitting in my usual spot, up in our one big tree on our land. It cradles me and forms to me like a chair, with comforting branches that listen to my thoughts. So many times it has heard me cry, laugh, sing, pray. Today I sit quietly, waiting to somehow hear an answer to my prayers, and I feel like God puts the Mercy Me song, "Keep Singing" in my mind where the singer talks about continuing on even through difficult times.

After hugging Aaron at graduation, and feeling him close to me again, I realized that I can't let him go so easily. I feel cold, even in the heat of the day, without him. I know in my heart, that he is truly supposed to be with me forever. I don't care that I'm only in high school. I *know* more than any other thing to be true, that he is my everything, and I am going to find a way to get him back, not just back to me, but back to himself, and back to his *real* family, the Alexanders.

Apparently Aaron finally confided in Jamie after graduation because Carla told me that Aaron is kind of on lock down at his house. Therefore, I will go to him. Since it's a weekend and summer, and since I'm almost another year older, Mom and Dad have agreed to let me go out with Carla and come home later than usual. As soon as Carla gets in my car, I am telling her my plan.

"Ok, so here's what we are going to do," I start.

"Dude, seriously, think about what happened last time you had some big plan and we ended up at that rickety, old house in town where Aaron's mom lives?"

"I know, but this time it won't be scary. He's at home, right? So there's nothing to be afraid of."

"Fine, but if we get in trouble, I'm totally kicking your butt," she says, grinning. I know she has my back no matter what, so she can talk all she wants.

We pick up Jamie and tell him the plan, and of course, he's all in. Aaron's house is five miles out of town, but it feels like it's taking us freakin' forever to get there. It's 10:00 at night, and I don't want to get him in trouble, so we turn our head lights off before getting too close to the house, and we park a little ways down the road so that our car can't be heard. It's go time.

It's pretty dark tonight. I guess the clouds are covering the moon, so I'm holding on to Carla who is holding on to Jamie as we quietly walk to where Aaron's window to his bedroom is. Once we get there, Jamie taps the window a couple of times. The lights are off, though, and there is no response, so Jamie taps the window again, this time a tiny bit louder. All of a sudden, we see what looks like a dim light come on, maybe to a cell phone or tablet or something. Then a flashlight shines right at us at the same time that the blinds open, and we all jump back, Carla and I gasping.

"Oh my gosh, Aaron! You scared the freakin' crap out of us!" I say.

"Whatever! Y'all are the crazy people who are sneaking around outside my house! Hello, don't you know I'm on lock-down?" he says, but smiles at the same time.

Gosh, I love his smile.

"What are y'all doing here?" he asks.

"Come out and we will tell you," Jamie says, but Aaron is too nervous to sneak out after everything that has happened lately, so he shakes his head, "Heck no, are y'all nuts?"

"Well, can you please tell us what is going on? How long are you stuck here? What's the deal with your bio parents?" we ask, all wondering the same things.

"Well, when you saw me the other day at the store, Mia, my dad was trying to make me steal some food. They found me the week after you and I were there, and I had to do things for them. Otherwise, they were going to hurt my family, hurt you. Dad knew you were more than a friend to me, Mia," he explains.

"Oh my gosh, Aaron! Why didn't you just talk to me?"

"Because, Mia! Do you really think you need to be around that? How would I protect you? They knew, Mia! They knew you were more to me, and there is no way in the world I would ever let you be near them again, not ever."

I stand there quietly, not knowing how to react. I'm so thankful and happy that he's finally talking to me and that it was because he cared about me that he distanced himself, but it still sucks.

"So, what now, Aaron? I hate the way things have been."

"I don't know. Obviously, I'm not going to just keep hiding out here. I'm freakin' 18. This is ridiculous! But, I am kind of thankful that my parents care enough about me to keep me safe. I know they mean well."

"Can we not just report your bio parents or something?" I ask, hoping there is some sort of easy resolution that we just haven't figured out yet.

"I don't know. My parents told me to trust them, so I'm trying to just chill out and do that. Please don't take this the wrong way, but you have to stay away, Mia. It's not ok for you to come back." He says this kind of sternly, and it makes me mad.

"Gosh, Aaron! I'm *so* sorry for caring about you and trying to help. Ugh!" I say, before telling Jamie and Carla to come on.

~~~~~~

One week later, I see on the news that Aaron's bio parents have been arrested for participating in a major drug ring. Apparently, they have been not only using meth and who knows what else, but they have been selling it again, too. *Ugh. They are so stupid. They deserve to be in jail forever!*

I text Aaron, "Saw the news. U ok?"

He replies, "I guess." It's pretty much a miracle that he finally replied to my text, even though he didn't exactly elaborate.

I don't know what to say to that, so I just text, "That's good."

He doesn't respond again. *Well, I guess that was that.*

My birthday is in five days. I think back on this year, and can't believe everything that has happened. I thought Aaron and I would be together right now, celebrating my birthday together again, but no, his stupid bio family had to ruin everything. I'm trying really hard to not be mad, but it's just not fair. Aaron deserves better, and so do I; so do *we*.

~~~~~~

I am so thankful to be going to church and to youth. I haven't gone to youth as much lately. I think I was just making excuses, but I told myself I was too busy with school work, or that I didn't want to go alone, or that I shouldn't use the gas to go back into town again. I've decided that the excuses will stop now. God has definitely answered my prayer to keep Aaron safe since his parents are now in jail where they need to be. Even if we aren't together, at least he's ok, which is the most important thing.

I went to youth early and filled Kathy in on all of the crazy drama that has unfolded in the last few months. Kathy listened and was very sweet, but she did tell me I have to forgive Aaron's bio parents, and that I need to be careful to not be ugly about them. She reminded me that Aaron still came from them, and that even if he doesn't act like them, he doesn't need to hear negative things about them. I understand and promise I will be careful with my tongue. The sermon today was about speaking life and not death, that there is power in the tongue, so I had already been thinking about how I could do better with what comes out of my mouth. I really do want to live for God.

Kathy prayed with me before other kids started showing up,

> *Dear Lord,*
>
> *We know You are in control, and that You know what is best. Romans 8:28 says that in all things, You will make it good. We trust You to do that, Father. We thank You and praise You, God, for keeping Aaron safe, and we ask You that You will continue to work in Aaron. Continue to help him find his identity and healing in You, God! We love You God! Thank You for your blessings, and thank You for Mia. Please bless her, too, and help guide her in every way. In Jesus' beautiful, Holy Name, Amen.*

"Amen," I agree, thinking about the power in that prayer. God is so awesome, and I am fired up.

~~~~~~~

I'm not having a big party this year for my birthday. Mom and Dad and Lily are planning to take me to eat at a nice restaurant in Crockett, and then I think Carla is going to spend the night. It's fine with me; it would be weird to have a huge party every year. I'm getting ready, and Lily is trying to convince me to wear a new skirt that I got for my birthday. I feel a little self-conscious in it because Lily and Mom picked it out for me, and it's different than what I would normally wear. It's really cute; it's just different. Lily has always had a super cute Indie style, but I never thought I could pull it off. This skirt is multi-colored and has faded-looking flowers on a white background. They got me a white, dressy spaghetti strap top to go with it, and it's supposed to be tucked in. Looking in the mirror, I know it looks cute, but I'm still lacking in confidence. *Oh well. It's not a big deal. We are just going to a restaurant, and it's not like people are going to care.*

I slip on my white, high-heeled sandals and grab my small matching cross-body purse so that I can carry my keys, cell phone, and tinted Chap Stick. I haven't had much need to fix up lately, so it's kind of fun to be able to feel different and cute.

We are at my favorite Italian restaurant, at a table in a little room in the back. It's cozy in here, with only four tables. The waiter is taking our drink orders when all of a sudden, I feel goosebumps all over my body, and I just know he's here. I can smell him, feel him, and my parents and Lily are looking past me, smiling.

I turn around to see Aaron walking in, flowers in one hand, and a Justin Beiber bag in the other. I can't help but laugh, but tears still fill my eyes when I see the most beautiful boy and the love of my life join us for my birthday, again.

"I can't believe you are here," I whisper to him as he comes up to the table.

"Is this seat taken?" he asks, pulling the chair next to me out from the table. He smiles, and I answer him with a slight shake of my head.

"How did you know we were here?" I ask.

"Your parents," he answers, grinning at them.

They just smile, and Mom even has tears in her eyes when she says, "We're so glad you could make it, Aaron!"

Aaron squeezes my leg under the table and hands me the flowers.

"They are beautiful!"

"Nothing compares to your beauty, Mia. You are beautiful inside and out, and I know that these flowers won't make up for everything that has happened, but I hope it's a start, babe."

Oh my gosh. Is this really happening? And he called me babe. I thought I would never hear that again.

"I love them, and I'm really happy you are here," I tell him.

Then he hands me the Justin Beiber bag. I giggle again, and thank him for knowing me so well and for thinking of me when he wrapped the present. Everyone at the table is laughing along with us, but when I pull out the present, it becomes quiet. Inside a tiny, adorable, box, is the most beautiful necklace that says, "Aaron" and then under that, it says, "Mia." There is a heart charm hanging alongside of it, and on the back, it says, "*Linked.*"

"Never again will we be apart, Mia. No matter what."

"I love it, Aaron, and I love you!" I hug him and say it again to make it more real, "I love you so much."

"I love you, too, Mia."

Dad clears his throat, causing us to snap out of our little moment, and we laugh and enjoy the rest of the evening. Carla was in on the whole surprise, too, so she isn't coming over tonight.

~~~~~~~

Once we are back home, in the comfort of Coyote, Aaron asks me to sit outside with him. I hear the familiar crickets and frogs chirping down by the small pond behind our house, and am filled with a peace that is all encompassing.

Aaron leads us to the swings, where we sit, hand in hand, just like last year. This year, though, we are closer, stronger, and I can feel the strength of our love is something that will never break apart again.

Aaron tells me, "I talked to Ken from church the other day."

"Really? But you haven't been to youth or anything."

"I know, but we had given each other our numbers a while back, and last week he texted me after seeing the crap on the news about my parents."

"Wow. That's nice. I know it bugs you to talk about it, but were you happy to hear from him?" I ask, unsure of how that would affect him.

"Actually, I really was. I have been trying so hard to get through this all alone, and even though I knew Ken grew up in a similar situation as me, I never really felt like he could possibly understand. Plus, the whole thing just sucks. It's embarrassing, ya know? I feel embarrassed that they were on the news and that I am their kid. I feel embarrassed that I fell for their stupid, freakin' lies again, and that I wasn't strong enough to just handle them myself," he tries to explain, his head down.

"Well, I don't think you need to be embarrassed. In fact, I'm really proud of you. You have come through a lot more than most people at this age, and you aren't doing the same bad things they were doing. You are a good person, Aaron."

"Thank you. I don't always feel like I am."

"So, what did Ken say anyway?" I ask, getting back to that.

"Well, we actually got together and went and got coffee together. He's really a pretty cool guy. It's not like he has all the answers or that he made me feel completely better, but it's nice that he can sort of understand what I've been going through. I just want to be able to get to the place where he is, confident that God is in control of things."

I nod my head and don't say anything, hoping he will continue to trust me enough to keep opening up to me.

"Anyway, it was good. He just said that I need to look at where I come from as being from God, not from my bio parents, or even my adoptive parents. He said it's about how we use our circumstances for God, and that it is our testimony, like how he's able to help me get through this because he's gone through it before. I want to do that for other kids now, too, even if it takes me a while to get to the place where I can."

"That's so awesome, Aaron. I'm so, so glad that he can be there for you. I mean, I don't wish what you have gone through on anyone, but think about how many kids have gone through similar stuff, are still going through it. I think it's so brave of you to even consider helping others, babe," I encourage him.

"Thank you, Mia. You know, I couldn't have gotten through all of this without you either. I started going to church because of you. You believed in me when I didn't even believe in myself, and even though I'm a work in progress, I feel like there is definitely hope. You are my light, babe, and I love you," he says, leaning over to kiss me. I answer with a smile.

It's kind of funny because I have been thinking a lot lately about how Aaron's adoption has affected him, and how Kathy talked about Aaron trying to find his true identity. After church the other night, I looked up "adoption" in my bible app, and this verse from Ephesians 1:3-6 came up in the Message version:

> How blessed is God! And what a blessing he is!
> He's the Father of our Master, Jesus Christ, and
> takes us to the high places of blessing in him.

> *Long before he laid down earth's foundations, he had us in mind, had settled on us as the focus of his love, to be made whole and holy by his love. Long, long ago he decided to adopt us into his family through Jesus Christ. (What pleasure he took in planning this!) He wanted us to enter into the celebration of his lavish gift-giving by the hand of his beloved Son.*

I am so thankful that God has not only brought Aaron and me closer together throughout this year but that He has brought both of us closer to Him. We are all adopted by God. Our true identity is in Him, which is the most amazing revelation to me. I say a silent prayer while sitting next to Aaron. I'm still not quite confident enough to pray out loud with him.

> *Lord, please let everyone on this earth feel Your presence and have a relationship with You, adopted by You. Use Aaron and me both for Your Kingdom. I praise Your Name, and thank You for blessing Aaron and me, and for bringing us closer to You. In Jesus' Name, Amen.*

As if he could hear my silent prayer, Aaron pulls our swings together and holds both chains with his hand, removing any distance between us.

Because, linked, we soar.

Acknowledgements

I would like to thank the following people: My husband, Jeremy, for loving and supporting me throughout this process, my mom, Linda, for her encouragement and help with formatting, my sister, Lori, and my friends Crystal, Cheryl, Kim, and Tina, for their detailed encouragement and feedback, Jacob and Leahnna for being models for the awesome cover, my cousin Angie for her support and for her mad editing skills, and my 9 children, who are my inspiring wild bunch.

Thank You, God, for giving me the words to write this novel. I pray that You will bless it and that it will be used to reach many, many people.

About the author

Elisa Ellis was born and raised in a small West Texas town. She married her high school sweetheart, Jeremy, and together, they raise their nine children. She briefly taught high school English before deciding to stay home with her kiddos, and has enjoyed a passion for photography and for writing.

Please visit my website, elisaellis.com, for more information.

Also, please review my book. I appreciate your incite and love feedback!

www.ingramcontent.com/pod-product-compliance
Lightning Source LLC
Chambersburg PA
CBHW020415150626
46554CB00014B/1634